More co
prepared

Okay, a man that droolworthy must not lack for female friends. So why had he been e-mailing her for two years? She wrinkled her nose, pushed her thick glasses back and studied him further.

Tight jeans, dirty boots. Long black hair under a black felt hat. Deep voice. Piercing eyes, she noted as he swung around, catching her staring at him. She jumped, he laughed and then he tipped his hat to her as he swung up onto an Appaloosa in a manner the stuntwoman in her appreciated.

Just how difficult would it be to entice that cowboy into her bed? Archer had put thoughts in her mind about his virility, with his Texas-sized bragging about his manliness and the babies popping out all over their ranch.

Seeing him, however, made her think that perhaps he hadn't been bragging as much as stating fact.

ABOUT THE AUTHOR

Tina Leonard loves to laugh, which is one of the many reasons she loves writing Harlequin American Romance books. In another lifetime, Tina thought she would be single and an East Coast fashion buyer forever. The unexpected happened when Tina met Tim again after many years—she hadn't seen him since they'd attended school together from first through eighth grade. They married, and now Tina keeps a close eye on her school-age children's friends! Lisa and Dean keep their mother busy with soccer, gymnastics and horseback riding. They are proud of their mom's "kissy books" and eagerly help her any way they can. Tina hopes that readers will enjoy the love of family she writes about in her stories. Recently a reviewer wrote, "Leonard has a wonderful sense of the ridiculous," which Tina loved so much she wants it for her epitaph. Right now, however, she's focusing on her wonderful life and writing a lot more romance!

Books by Tina Leonard

ARCHER'S ANGELS
Tina Leonard

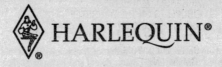

HARLEQUIN®

TORONTO • NEW YORK • LONDON
AMSTERDAM • PARIS • SYDNEY • HAMBURG
STOCKHOLM • ATHENS • TOKYO • MILAN • MADRID
PRAGUE • WARSAW • BUDAPEST • AUCKLAND

ISBN 0-373-75057-9

ARCHER'S ANGELS

Copyright © 2005 by Tina Leonard.

This edition published by arrangement with Harlequin Books S.A.

® and TM are trademarks of the publisher. Trademarks indicated with ® are registered in the United States Patent and Trademark Office, the Canadian Trade Marks Office and in other countries.

www.eHarlequin.com

Printed in U.S.A.

THE JEFFERSON BROTHERS
OF MALFUNCTION JUNCTION

Mason (38), Maverick and Mercy's eldest son—He can't run away from his own heartache or The Family Problem.

Frisco Joe (37)—Fell hard for Annabelle Turnberry and has sweet Emmie to show for it. They live in Texas wine country.

Fannin (36)—Life can't be better than cozying up with Kelly Stone and his darling twins in Ireland.

Laredo (35), twin to Tex—Loves Katy Goodnight, North Carolina and being the only brother with a reputation for winning his woman without staying on a bull.

Tex (35), twin to Laredo—Grower of roses and other plants, Tex fell for Cissy Kisserton and decided her water-bound way of life was best.

Calhoun (34)—Doesn't want the family mantle passing to him.

Ranger (33), twin to Archer—Fell for Hannah Hotchkiss and will never leave the open road without her.

Archer (33), twin to Ranger—Talking with a faraway woman in Australia by e-mail is better than having a real woman to bother him.

Crockett (31), twin to Navarro—Paints portraits of nudes, but never wants to see a woman fully clothed in a wedding gown saying, "I do" to him.

Navarro (31), twin to Crockett—Fell for Nina Cakes when he was supposed to be watching her sister, Valentine, who is carrying Last's child.

Bandera (27)—Spouts poetry and has moved from Whitman to Frost—anything to keep his mind off the ranch's troubles.

Last (26)—The only brother who finds himself expecting a baby with no hope of marrying the mother. Will he ever find the happy ending he always wanted?

To Nicki and Jason Flockton, for kindly sharing their love and their excitement over their children with me and our friends, the Gal Pals. Your joy was inspiring.

Much love to my children, Lisa and Dean. Don't leave me too soon—I'm enjoying you too much.

And heartfelt gratitude to my editors, Paula Eykelhof and Stacy Boyd, whose belief in this series has meant so much to me.

Prologue

Love at first sight? Yes. Love over time? Yes. But there are no shortcuts to the heart.
—Maverick to his sons one night, after their mother had passed, when they wondered how a man ever knew he'd found the one woman for him

From: TexasArcher
To: AussieClove
Howdy, AussieClove. What's shaking Down Under? I just got home from riding a bull at the rodeo in Lonely Hearts Station. After the events me and some of my bros decided to drink some of the wildest concoction on the planet. We ended up baying at the moon beside Barmaid's Creek, with some crazy gals for company. You should have seen me ride that bull—if he hadn't come back around to the left, I would have been the first brother in my family to stay on that cursed piece of cowhide, Bloodthirsty Black.

From: AussieClove
To: TexasArcher
G'day, TexasArcher. Nothing shaking here except maybe my head. My older sister, Lucy, is devastated tonight. She and her husband have learned they can probably never have children. So I threw myself into work, hoping to stay positive.

The stunt tonight involved a boat, some fire, a shark and two guys wearing what I would call thongs. I think guys should never wear swim clothes that are smaller than their...well, you know. What do cowboys wear under those Wrangler jeans?

From: TexasArcher
To: AussieClove
Man alive, AussieClove. Sorry to hear about your sister—that's too bad. Around our ranch, we're having a population explosion. We've got babies popping out all over the place. I'm never having kids. In fact, I'm never getting married. Too complicated.

One time, I was stuck in a truck with my twin brother, Ranger, and his now-wife, Hannah, and they griped at each other for days. I finally escaped, but Ranger wasn't so lucky. He rolled down an arroyo and demanded that a medicine man marry him and Hannah because he was convinced he had to get married to live. My twin's weird. By the way, I wear briefs and sometimes nothing. What do Aussie girls wear under

their clothes? (I can tell you right now, floss-size draw-
ers would never hold everything of mine.)

From: AussieClove
To: TexasArcher
I'm sure.☺

Chapter One

Clove Penmire's heart pounded as she got off the bus in Lonely Hearts Station, Texas, suitcase in hand. For all her fascination with cowboys and the lure of the dusty state she'd read so much about, she had to admit small-town Texas was nothing like her homeland of Australia.

A horse broke free from the barn across the street, walking itself nonchalantly between the two sides of the old-time town. A cowboy sprinted out of the barn and ran up the street after his horse, laughing as he caught up to it.

Clove smiled. From the back she couldn't tell if the man was handsome, but he was dressed in Wrangler jeans and a hat, and, as far as she could tell, the cowboy was the real thing.

That's what she had traveled to Texas for: the real thing.

That sentiment would have sounded shallow, even to Clove, just a month ago. But having learned that her sister, Lucy, could not have a child, Clove's thought processes had taken a new course, one that included fantasies of tossing her brother-in-law into the Australian ocean.

All over the world there were people who couldn't conceive when they wished. They adopted, or pursued other means of happiness. She hadn't been overly worried, until Lucy confessed that she thought her husband might leave her for a woman who could bear children.

Lucy had laughed a little sadly and said that perhaps she was only imagining things. Clove had murmured something reassuring, but inside, fear struck her. Lucy loved her physician husband. He'd always seemed to adore her. Men didn't leave women because they couldn't bear children, did they? Robert was a wonderful man; Clove had been surprised, and distressed, at the turn of events.

So she'd taken drastic measures. She'd come to America for Archer Jefferson.

The cowboy hauled his horse around, leading it back toward the barn. Clove could hear him lightly remonstrating his wayward beast, but the horse didn't seem too concerned.

The cowboy caught her interested gaze, holding it for a second before he looked back at his horse. The man was extremely handsome. Breathtakingly so. Not the cowboy for her, considering her mission, and the fact that she was what people politely referred to as…the girl with the good personality.

The girl everybody loved like a sister.

The girl men liked to be friends with.

And the worst, the Nerdy Penmire.

She sighed. If Lucy had gotten all the beauty, their mother always said with a gentle smile, then Clove had gotten all the bravery. Which was likely how she'd ended up as a stuntwoman.

A stuntwoman with thick glasses.

Had she the face of other Australian exports like Nicole Kidman, for example, she might have been in front of the camera. But instead, she was a stunt double. Lucy said Clove had the life other people dreamed of.

Maybe.

Clove watched the cowboy brush his horse's back with his hand and fan a fly away from its spot-marked face. He was still talking to the animal; she could hear low murmuring that sounded very sexy to her ears, especially since she'd never heard a man murmur in a husky voice to her.

"Archer Jefferson!" someone yelled from inside the barn. "Get that cotton-pickin', apple-stealin', dog-faced Appaloosa in here!"

"Insult the man but not the sexy beast!" he yelled back.

Clove gasped. Archer Jefferson! The man she'd traveled several time zones to see! Her TexasArcher of two years' worth of e-mail correspondence!

He was all cowboy, she realized, more cowboy than she'd come mentally prepared to corral. "Whoa," she murmured to herself.

Okay, a man that droolworthy must not lack for female friends. So why had he been writing her for two years? She wrinkled her nose, pushed her thick glasses back and studied him further. Tight jeans, dirty boots. Long, black, unkempt hair under the black felt hat— he'd never mentioned long hair in their correspondence.

Deep voice. Piercing eyes, she noted as he swung around, catching her still staring at him. She jumped, he laughed, and then tipped his hat to her as he swung up onto the "dog-faced" Appaloosa, riding it into the barn in a manner the stuntwoman in her appreciated.

Just how difficult would it be to entice that cowboy into her bed? Archer had put the thoughts in her mind about his virility, with his Texas-size bragging about his manliness and the babies popping out all over their Union Junction ranch—affectionately known as Malfunction Junction.

Seeing him, however, made her think that perhaps he hadn't been bragging as much as stating fact. Her heart beat faster. He had said he wasn't in the market for a relationship.

But a baby, just one baby…one stolen seed from a family tree that bore many…from a man she trusted more than a stranger from a sperm bank.

Maybe she *wasn't* brave.

"Howdy!"

She jumped as Archer strode across the street to where she stood.

"Are you lost?" he asked.

"No," she said, her gaze taking in every inch of him with nervous admiration. "Yes."

He grinned. "My name's Archer Jefferson."

She wished he wouldn't smile at her that way. Her heart simply melted, despite the cold chill of February. He made her dream of a blazing fireplace, soft blankets and naked him holding naked her tight.

"Can I help you?" he asked. "If you're looking for a job, the cafeteria is that way. If you're looking for a hair-do," he said, eyeing her braided hair momentarily, "I'd choose that salon over there. The Lonely Hearts Salon. Owner's a friend of mine. Salon owner across the street, of the Never Lonely Cut-n-Gurls, isn't."

She felt him studying her glasses, the cursed thick things that gave her clear vision when she was doing stunts. Contacts made her eyes itch and burn.

Lucy said Clove hid behind her glasses. Clove blinked, thinking that right now a curtain was the only thing she'd feel truly hidden behind.

"You sure are a quiet little thing," Archer said. "Don't be scared. We're all real friendly here."

Scared! She was a daredevil!

But if she told him that, in her lilting Aussie accent, he would know who she was right off. And he would think she was nuts for coming all the way to Texas without telling him. He would know it was no accident that she was standing outside the rodeo he had told her he was participating in.

"I'm not scared," she said, trying to disguise her accent. "Thank you for your concern."

"Ah, she speaks," Archer said. "I've got to run, but if you need anything, just grab someone off the street to help you. This is a friendly town, if you bypass the Cut-n-Gurls."

"I'll do that."

He tipped his hat, and with a flash of long-legged denim glory, he disappeared into the arena building.

Her breath slowly left the cage it was bound in.

No doubt his genes were as sexy as his jeans. He was far hotter than the thong-wearing models she'd last worked with.

Now she just had to get those jeans off of him.

He hadn't seemed particularly inclined to strip down to the "briefs or nothing" of which he'd boasted. Not even a flash of male attraction had lit his eye. "I don't know if I can do this," she murmured, suddenly doubtful about her mission.

He was terribly manly. And she had very little experience with men. Lucy had always been the one who warmed to hearth and home.

Clove took a deep breath. For Lucy's sake, she had to be brave.

She went into the walkway where Archer had disappeared. He was leaning against a rail, looking at his Appaloosa. Seeing her, he grinned. "Glad you came in. I was just thinking you might need a hotel."

Her throat gulped of its own accord. "Ah," she said, "I was wondering…"

"Yes?" he said, smiling down at her.

He was so tall. "Would you care to go to dinner with me?" she asked, her voice barely a whisper.

The friendly smile slipped from his face. His gaze touched her glasses. Then a forced veneer of friendliness came back to his expression. "I'm sorry. I can't."

She blinked, knowing her face was bright red.

"Okay. Thanks, anyway."

Backing away, she saw sympathy in his gaze.

She turned and tried to walk away with as much dignity as possible. He was not remotely interested. How humiliating!

This was not going to be easy. In fact, it likely was impossible.

On the other hand, she was a stuntwoman known for her never-fail nerves. And she hadn't paid for a round-trip airline ticket to wind up going back home without a Texas-bred souvenir.

For Lucy's sake, she would bring out the daredevil residing inside her and let it loose all over that cowboy.

ARCHER JEFFERSON watched the little fraidy-cat walk away with some regret. My goodness, she was a shy one! Traveling by herself required some bravery, though.

If he had a rule—and usually he didn't—it was that most women were to be avoided. He'd learned from watching his brothers fall that women came in exciting, colorful packages; some fun to open, some not. But a shy woman didn't hold much threat to his well-being. And that one, with her oversize specs and timid little voice couldn't put fear into a flea.

Scratching his head, he thought about her dinner invitation. Much as he might have enjoyed showing a newcomer the town, he had to get his horse ready for the show. Honky-Tonk was a tricky Appaloosa. She thought she knew things she didn't, and they'd had more than one disagreement between them about who was boss.

"You're just a bit sassy," he said to Tonk. "You think

you're entitled to your own opinions. But we both know better, don't we?"

She pinned an ear back and gave him a sidelong stare.

"Females and opinions go together like butter and bread," he continued.

And it often seemed as if his Appaloosa had her fair share of womanly arts, conniving and one-upping being some of them. He knew quite well that females had a spectrum of tricks up their dainty sleeves. He'd watched seven brothers before him fall prey to the wedding-ring chase.

The last brother who'd fallen was Calhoun. He'd settled at the ranch, the first married brother to do so. Calhoun had brought his wife's family—two children, Minnie and Kenny, and a grandfather, Barley—with him.

And Calhoun's success had generated some brotherly angst around the ranch. Calhoun had the kids, the father-in-law, the occasional roadshow participation as a rodeo clown—for which his wife, Olivia, adored him—but Calhoun had also became a hit with his paintings. Though he'd started out painting nudes, he had switched to family portraits and had a waiting list of people who wanted him to commit their children to canvas.

He was that good.

Unfortunately, Crockett, the family's first and best artist, had taken umbrage at this. Crockett felt Calhoun had one-upped him in the creative department. Archer frowned as he worked his way through the mud in Tonk's hoof. Usually, the brothers were happy for each other. But ever since the youngest brother, Last, had brought a new baby to the ranch, along with the baby's unmarried mother, Valentine, no one had been happy.

Or maybe the trouble had started when Mason left. Oldest brother, and patriarch of the Jefferson clan, he'd taken his wandering feet onto the road. He'd said he wanted to find out what had happened to their father, Maverick. But the brothers knew that was a lie; Mason had been nearly knocked to his knees when Mimi Cannady, their next-door neighbor, married another man and had a baby.

But that had been more than a year ago. Mimi and Brian were divorced now, a friendly divorce. And Mason had returned and was now very fond of one-year-old, Nanette.

Archer sighed. Maybe all the craziness around Malfunction Junction was just the result of twelve brothers growing up together with no female touch to soften them.

Last was never going to settle down with Valentine, though he seemed to be receiving better marks for his daddy skills.

Mason was never going to get his head straight about Mimi. All the brothers *except* Mason knew Mimi was putting her ranch up for sale in order to move into town.

Bandera never shut up about poetry. He wrote it, he sang it, he reviewed it and recited it, and if he didn't shut his face, Archer was going to smother him in his sleep.

Crockett needed to just shut his yap and paint. There was room for two artists in the family tree.

"I'm the only brother who keeps my pipe shut," Archer told Tonk. "My insanity is on the down-low. I write a woman who is far away and who will never bother me. As far as I can see, I add no turbulence to this family ship. Why can't the rest of my brothers be more suave? Debonair?"

It sounded as if Tonk groaned. He gave her a tap on the fanny. "Hey," he said, "no comments from you. Or maybe I won't defend you the next time my brothers call you dog-faced." He frowned, looking at the pretty colors of his spotted equine. She was beautiful! What was it about her that they didn't get? So Tonk was a little unusual. Archer liked unusual things.

She reached out with her back hoof, not really kicking at him but giving him a little goose. He stepped back, eyeing her warily. *"Tonk,"* he said, his tone warning.

She flipped her mane at him.

"Excuse me," he heard.

Archer glanced up to see the little plain newcomer looking at him. "Yes?"

"I was just offered employment at the Never Lonely Cut-n-Gurls Salon."

"You were?" Straightening, he stared at her.

Marvella, the owner of the Never Lonely Cut-n-Gurls, was always on the lookout for fresh stylists, and Marvella's stylists were known far and wide to be babes—and if they weren't babes, then they were possessed of supernatural talents. If you were a man, the Cut-n-Gurls could *always* help you out.

"Yes." She nodded. "But I knew you said they weren't your friends."

"They're not, that's true. What is it that you do?" he

asked, staring at her speculatively. Maybe there was more to her than he'd first thought. Marvella had a pretty good eye for these things.

"I—I'm not doing anything right now," she said. "I'm on vacation."

"So, what did you tell her?" Archer felt worry assail him. Employment with Marvella included hassles, so many she'd soon dream of giving back her wages.

"I told her, no, thank you. You said to avoid her."

"I think it would be best. Not that I'm always right."

She nodded. "Even your horse knows that."

Archer frowned. "What do you mean?"

She shrugged. "She doesn't like you."

He was outraged. "She likes me fine!"

She shook her head. "No, see how she distances herself from you? She thinks you're bossy. Trying to enforce yourself upon her."

His jaw dropped. "She's a horse. I'm *supposed* to enforce myself upon her."

"She doesn't like it. She's trying to tell you that you're annoying."

Well, that was it. He didn't have to listen to some half-baked claptrap like that. Tonk and he had a special relationship.

"How long have you had her?"

"Tonk and I have been together six months," Archer said defensively. "And Tonk thinks I'm—"

"Bossy." She reached a hand over the stall, and Tonk slid her nose under the woman's fingers. "I understand, girl. Men can be very trying."

"Are you trying to do that horse-talking thing?" Archer asked. "I don't use horse psychology. I mean, I talk to Tonk, but I'm really just amusing myself. I don't believe we're actually *communicating*—"

Her eyebrows raised. She stared at him, her gaze challenging. Disbelieving?

Something about that attitude caught Archer's attention. He looked at her more closely, finally seeing behind the specs.

"Those are beautiful eyes you're hiding."

Chapter Two

"Thank you," Clove said, "I think."

He looked at her. "No, really. You have lovely eyes. Very unique color."

She was torn between feeling flattered, giving in to worry, or pulling out her tricks. He was, after all, the key player in her plan.

"What's your name, stranger?" he asked.

"Clover," she said, thinking quickly, not yet ready to reveal her identity.

"Clover? Is that a real name or are you making one up just to keep your distance?"

"It's a real name." Just not hers.

He frowned. "You don't look like a Clover."

"I'd ask you what I do look like, but I don't want to know." She leaned over into the stall. "Oh, Tonk has blue hooves," she said. "I think blue hooves on a horse are so pretty."

He narrowed his gaze on her. "Know a little something about horses, do you?"

"A little. My family owns a farm." Clove glanced up at him. "We raise horses."

"Oh? Where's the farm? The Jeffersons know just about everyone in the business."

"Well, you wouldn't know us," Clove said. "Our farm is not doing as well as one might hope."

"Sorry to hear that." He turned his attention back to Tonk, who was still nuzzling at Clove's fingers.

"Oh, Archer!" Feminine voices floated into the stall.

Clove turned to see four beautiful girls walk by with flirtatious glances for Archer. She turned back around in time to see Archer's chest puff out about four inches.

"Hey, ladies," he called. "Nice winter weather, huh?"

They giggled. "We've got some hot cocoa when you feel like warming up," one girl said.

Another nodded. "And some of our special potion tastes good on a freezing night. Madame Mystery's—"

"Yes, yes," Archer said hurriedly. He waved them on. "You girls behave. Get inside before you all catch colds."

Laughing, they waved mittened fingers at him and moved on after casting him one last alluring glance.

Clove blinked. "They practically undressed you en masse."

He laughed. "Yeah. They're good at that."

And he had no shame! Clove quickly reviewed her position. Maybe *mano a mano* she could get his attention, but groupie corralling put the odds against her. Not to mention that those women were gorgeous.

"They mean no harm," he said easily, "as long as they get no closer than about ten feet."

"How do you know?"

He winked at her. "Women are not hard to figure out."

She held back a gasp at his cockiness. "You haven't figured out your horse."

"And that's why I love only her." He gave Tonk an affectionate pat on the shoulder, and she tried to nail him with a hoof. Swiftly jumping forward, he dodged the hoof, but Tonk's head snaked around, her teeth barely missing his shoulder.

"I guess you'd call that a love peck," Clove said.

"Aw, Tonk wouldn't really bite me. She just knows I like a little sauce to my women."

"Women?"

He grinned, pushing his hat back with a finger.

He was annoying, and much sexier than he'd come across in his e-mails. She needed a shower to freshen up after her travels, and time to regroup. "I think I'll be going now," she said, retreating from his confident smile.

"Thanks for the dinner offer," he said, "But Tonk and I have work to do."

Now that she'd seen him turn down the quartet of country lovelies, her feelings weren't quite so hurt, so she was able to flip him a shrug. "About that hotel you were going to recommend?"

"There's no hotel in Lonely Hearts Station, but both beauty salons welcome travelers. Head over to the Lonely Hearts Salon. The owner, Delilah, has rooms for rent. You'll be safe over there." His gaze settled on Clove for a moment, then he put the horse's hoof down and came over to the rail, leaning on it to stare down at her. "Do not take a room at the Never Lonely Cut-n-Gurls salon. Even though you will see a big sign out front proclaiming that theirs are the cheapest, cleanest, most comfortable rooms in town."

She backed away from his intensity. "You are quite forceful, sir."

"Yeah, well, someone's gotta be around here." He turned back to his horse. "Otherwise we'd all be love candy for women and ending up at the gooey altar of marriage."

Whew! He was simply brewing in misery when it came to women, Clove realized. In their e-mails, he'd always made everything sound so wonderful, so care-free, so…fairy tale. But in person, the story was quite different.

"Good luck," she said, backing away, "with your rodeo. Or whatever it is that you're after."

He waved a hand absently.

Clove waved a hand back, mimicking him, but he never noticed. She went out onto the pavement, crossing her arms against the chill.

It was true what Archer said. There was a large sign out in front of the Never Lonely salon. In fact, the whole building was lit up with white lights, like icing on a gingerbread house. Laughter floated from inside, and a piano gaily played ragtime.

She glanced across the street at the Lonely Hearts Salon. A lamp glowed in the window, and it was mostly dark and very quiet, as if no one ever stayed there.

She turned back to the Never Lonely salon. Four really pretty, lively women who knew how to get Archer's attention lived inside. And hadn't those flirty girls said something about hot cocoa?

Clove shivered. She wasn't used to this kind of cold.

The cocoa—and the chance to get some advice on how to seduce her man—won out. She headed toward the Never Lonely Cut-n-Gurls Salon.

ARCHER WAITED until he heard Clover walking away, then he turned to stealthily watch her leave. Nice fanny, for a girl with a plain face and wacky glasses. She was packing her jeans just fine. He liked her voice, too, he had to admit. It was very sweet, with a slight accent.

"You embarrassed me, Tonk," he said. "Could you at least go easy on me in front of girls? You make me look like I'm the hoss and you're the rider."

Tonk ignored him.

"Hey!" Bandera came and leaned his elbows over the rail. "Let's eat. I'm hungry. Hey, what's up with Dog-face? Someone feed her a sour apple?"

"Shut up." Archer put away the hoof pick and other tack. "There was a girl here a second ago—"

"Oh, is that your problem?"

"And she went to find a room, I think."

"Ah." Bandera nodded knowingly. "And you want the key."

"No! She's not…my type." He glanced at his brother. "I told her to go over to Delilah's."

"Yeah?" Bandera laughed. "If she was that girl in glasses I just saw, then she's just like your horse."

Archer straightened. "Meaning?"

"Meaning she doesn't mind very well. She went straight to Marvella's."

"What? I specifically told her—"

Bandera grinned. "Archer, if you had a Dear Abby column, you'd go broke. No one listens to you."

Archer ignored him. "That crazy girl has no idea what she's getting herself into!"

"Well, don't get too worried about it."

Archer settled his hat on his head. "Someone has to look out for the misfits in life. And if there ever was a misfit, Clover is her."

"Whoa. Color me *impressed*."

Archer slapped his brother upside the head. "Come on. We've got to catch her before she gets too far into the dragon's den!"

CLOVE COULD NOT IMAGINE why Archer had steered her away from surely the nicest girls on the planet. Taking pity on her plight—poor, tired traveler!—they'd treated her to a wonderful array of services.

They'd coaxed her glasses from her, leaving her nearly blind. They'd teased and washed her hair. Perfumed her. Stuck some heels on her feet. Given her a knockout dress to wear, the type of thing one saw on elegant ladies.

She'd been a bit embarrassed, but they'd waved aside her worries. It was all part of the service, Marvella said. Besides, Clove was renting a room, and that more than covered the expense. And gave her girls some practice with a lady's hair, since they mostly had male clients.

"Can I have my glasses for just one sec?"

Marvella handed them to her. Clove put them on so she could peer in the mirror. "Oh, my," she said. "I had no idea I could look like this."

"It was all there," Marvella said. "Hidden charms. The best kind, I always say. I had another girl, once upon a time. You remind me of her. By the time I got done with her, she was a golden charm. She left me," Marvella said bitterly. "Ah well, that's in the past."

"What was her name?" Clove asked, out of politeness more than curiosity. It was clear Marvella wanted to draw out the girl chat a bit more.

"Cissy. Cissy…Kisserton. Now Jefferson."

"Jefferson?"

Marvella nodded. "Those damn Jeffersons get all my girls. They've got Valentine right now, and not one of them has any intention of marrying her."

Clove sucked in her breath. "What do you mean, *they've got her?*"

"One of the brothers impregnated her, another took her to their ranch, and they've kept her there. After she gave birth they put her to work in a bakery."

Clove's eyes were huge. "That sounds *terrible.*"

"It is. If you ever meet a Jefferson man, my best advice to you is *run.*"

Clove blinked. That was the same thing Archer had said about the Never Lonely Cut-n-Gurls! "I'm still confused about the plural," she said.

"Oh, you'd find quick enough that the Jeffersons do everything as a gang, a fixture upon our good and tidy landscape that can't be overlooked, an eyesore, if you will. They approach you in a group. If one of them is alone, soon enough they'll have backup. Before you know it, you're theirs."

Clove could hardly take this in. She thought about Archer's hot, lean physique and felt her breath catch in her chest. "It sounds…"

"Scary, I know."

Clove had been working the adjective "romantic" over in her mind. Hot. Sexy. Fantastic…

Marvella clucked with sympathy. "Don't you worry about a thing. I have my dealings with the Jeffersons as necessary, but one thing is certain—they will never, ever take one of my girls from me again. And right now, you're one of *my* girls."

"Thank you." Now was the wrong time to mention that she'd actually come to town to shanghai some Jefferson genes.

"How can I ever thank you for all you've done for me?" she quietly asked Marvella.

"You sit here," Marvella said, "right up front, my precious, and just smile for the customers who come in the door. Just an hour," she said, "will be repayment enough."

"You could not have possibly seen Clover go into Marvella's," Archer told Bandera. "I have seven-eight brother syndrome, which means I'm so far down on the family tree that I have to be observant or I get run over by my own beloved brothers. And I distinctly saw Clover turn left as she left the pens."

"She may have," Bandera said agreeably. "You may have seven-eight brother syndrome, but I have eleventh-brother syndrome, which means I was so close to becoming Last that I make certain everything is proven fact before I talk about it. And I saw a lady who looked a little hesitant, with big ugly glasses, go into Marvella's."

Archer's boots moved faster as he headed to the door of the salon. "You're crazy. She said she would listen to me. Good evening, miss," he said, tipping his hat to the gorgeous woman seated on a bar stool just inside the doorway.

She stared at him, not inclined to say much, he guessed. Glancing around for Clover, he turned back to the bar-stool babe. "Did you happen to see a woman come in here, one who was lost, wearing glasses as thick as the tires on a truck?"

She looked perplexed, then she shook her head. He glanced over her big hair and her superbly applied makeup. The wooden bar stool only served to enhance her hourglass shape, keeping the focus on her curves as she sat straight for balance.

"You see," he told Bandera, "Clover would stick out in here like a barn owl amongst peacocks. Let's go check with Delilah." He tipped his hat to the babelicious door greeter and headed out.

"Man alive, she was hot as a smokin' pistol!" Bandera exclaimed. "Have you noticed that Marvella's girls just keep getting hotter and hotter? Whooee! I feel like someone just lit a firecracker in my jeans!"

"She was all right," Archer said. "Actually, she reminded me of Cissy. And you know, I love our sister-in-law, but remember, I was stuck in a truck once upon a time with her and Hannah, and I'm telling you, girls who look like that are *misfired* pistols in the wrong hands."

"My hands would be just right," Bandera said. "Oh, how quickly I would volunteer to be her bar stool the next time she needed a place to park that fanny!"

"Dunce," Archer told him. "Get a grip. We've got a tourist to rescue." They went across the street to Delilah's, quietly tapping on the door because of the hour. The Jeffersons had their own keys for the back door, where they could go up the stairs and commandeer a special set of rooms Delilah kept just for them. But right now, Archer was hoping for intel on his lost farm girl.

"Why are you so worried about her, anyway?" Bandera demanded. "Let's go back over to Marvella's and spark a fire with the damsels."

"No hunting for trouble tonight," Archer stated. "If we bring home any more bad news related to Marvella, Mason'll probably run us out of town for good. He still can't believe Last got one of her girls pregnant while Mason was gone."

They peered through the curtained window of the front door. Only a quaint lamp burned on the table. "Guess she and Jerry called it an early night," Archer said. "Darn."

"That means your little friend isn't here. Delilah would be bustling around in the kitchen, making her welcome."

"That's true." Now Archer was extremely worried.

"Could I be mistaken?" Bandera asked. "Perhaps I didn't see her go into Marvella's, and in fact, she has left town."

Archer wheeled to look at him. "*Are* you mistaken?"

"If I say I am, can we go hit on Miss February over at Marvella's?"

"No!" Archer was good and put out with his brother. "How can you think of women at a time like this! There is a poor girl somewhere in this town who has no place to go, and all you can think about is your…you know." He wished it didn't bother him so much that Clover might have left town. Certainly he had not been very friendly. "Just so long as she didn't go to Marvella's, I really don't care where she went. That's all I'm doing, trying to keep an innocent traveler from getting fleeced."

"That's right." Bandera nodded. "That's all that's on your mind. And I'm not thinking about that beauty on the bar stool at all!"

CLOVE COULDN'T BELIEVE that Archer had left without recognizing her. It was so exciting! She felt like a different girl.

She was completely new.

The thought made her bite her lip. Clove felt her puffed-up big hair and her mascaraed lashes. The look really wasn't her, though it was fun. But in a while, her eyes would start to itch from the makeup, and anyway, her scalp felt tight from all the hair spray lacquered onto her head.

She was glad he didn't know she'd run counter to his suggestion and come to Marvella's.

One hour had passed, the allotted time Marvella had asked her to sit out front. Longing for a shower, Clove went upstairs to her new room, closing the door. The feminine side of her wished Archer had noticed the big change in her—and the practical side remembered that he'd noticed her less as Cinderella than he had when she'd been Plain Jane.

It was time to let the inner stuntwoman in her throw caution to the wind.

Surely it couldn't be that hard to attract a man.

"Yoo-hoo!" a voice called.

"Come in!"

One of the stylists walked into her room, leaving a small bottle on the table. "Marvella wants you to have some of her delicious home brew as a welcome gift."

"That's so kind. She's already done too much."

The stylist smiled. "She must like you."

Clove looked at the bottle. "Hey, a cowboy came in here tonight. His name was Archer Jefferson. Do you know him?"

"Know him?" The woman laughed. "We know *all* the Malfunction Junction boys. Why?"

"Just wondering."

"If you're thinking he's cute, so does every woman in this place. But don't spend too much time thinking about him. That one is impossible. All he cares about is his horse, ugly dog that she is."

Clove frowned. Tonk was beautiful in her own way.

"But if you just can't live without him, you'll probably find him at Delilah's. I'd head up the back stairs if I were you, because Delilah won't welcome you if she knows you're staying here. Tap on the door, say 'room service,' and see if he's hungry."

"You make it sound so easy," Clove murmured.

"Trust me, it's not. Good luck, though." She laughed again and left the room.

Clove stared at the closed door, then at the bottle on the nightstand. The stylist's words ran through her brain, a mockery of her intentions.

One thing was for certain, she wasn't going to use alcohol to lure a man into her bed. And right now, she was going to shower all this hair spray and makeup off her body. She felt like a doll.

And then, if a shower hadn't washed all the thoughts of Archer out of her mind, surely it wouldn't hurt to go across the street and take a look at the back door the stylist had mentioned.

Not that she would go in, of course. But curiosity had her, and she wouldn't be a stuntwoman if she wasn't up for a dare.

Chapter Three

Archer couldn't sleep, though Bandera was sawing logs like a frontiersman. "I just need to walk it off," he muttered to himself. "I've got nerves before the big show, and I'm worrying about Clover so I don't worry about Tonk."

Neither of the females on his mind obeyed worth a flip, not that he would admit that to Bandera. One thing he did know about Clover—if she was the sort of girl who understood that a man knew best, she'd be under Delilah's roof right now.

Where he could keep an eye on her.

So he took a few laps up and down the main street of Lonely Hearts Station, his gaze darting, ever-watchful, for the traveler who knew about blue hooves. Tonk sure had seemed to like Clover, which was strange, because Tonk didn't like anyone, a fact his brothers were quick to point out, and which Archer was quicker to deny.

He was certain Tonk held affection for him somewhere in her equine heart. She just didn't know how to show it. He'd been told by plenty of women that he didn't know how to show affection to a woman, either, so that made he and Tonk a perfect pair.

Archer was so busy ruminating on the canny females in his life that he nearly got too close to the one peering in the back window of the Lonely Hearts Salon. It was Clover!

She was spying, the little peeping Tomasina.

Or maybe she didn't know how to get in. Perhaps she'd decided to take his advice.

He watched her carefully turn the doorknob and open the door. She appeared to think about something for a second, then closed the door. She opened the door, and closed it again.

Spying. Which meant, he knew with certain chauvinism, that she wanted to spy on *him.*

He grinned, knowing exactly what to do with her now. Sneaking up on her, he reached out and grabbed her around the waist. "Gotcha!" he roared.

She screamed, kicking back with her feet—just like Tonk, dammit—giving him a crotch-kick that left him clutching for air. She pounced, knocking him back onto the ground. Like a helpless puppy he lay there, focusing on the stars in the black-velour sky above, wondering if he was ever going to be able to draw breath again.

"Archer!" she cried. "I didn't know it was you!"

Groaning, he rolled onto his side.

"Are you all right?" she asked. "Here, lie on your back so you can get your breath."

"Uh-huh," he said on a strangled moan. "Don't move an injured man."

"I didn't hurt your back," she said reasonably. "Or your neck. You'll be all right in a minute. You just need to relax. Relax, Archer."

"Lucky for me I didn't want kids," Archer said, "because you just kicked in any chance I ever had of dispatching 'em."

"What?"

He rolled his eyes at her tone. Maybe he shouldn't speak so in front of a lady, but she needed to quit trying to roll him over. He wanted to curl up and think about tomorrow—surely the pain would be gone by then. "You just made me the first Jefferson male who won't need birth control."

"Oh, no. Archer, don't even joke about that! You sit right up, catch your breath and…maybe we should take your jeans off. Would that help? I read somewhere that jeans cut down on a man's, uh, sperm motility, due to the warmth and constricting nature of the fabric."

She was crazy, he'd admit that. "Thank you, I'm fine. Though I didn't want to end my child-giving days quite that way, I'll admit one swift kick was probably as good as paying some doctor quack to do it."

"You want to have as many children as you possibly can!"

"Don't think I will now that my factory's gone crooked. Help me to my feet."

"I will not. You lie there while I go for help."

"No!" That was the last thing he wanted—everyone in Lonely Hearts and Union Junction knowing that a woman had disarmed him. "Hey, where'd you go tonight?"

"Shh," she told him. "Don't talk. Just think happy thoughts. Happy, healing, healthy thoughts. Big, Jefferson-male-testosterone thoughts."

"There's nothing wrong with my testosterone," he grumbled, "just the delivery system. Move, okay? You're treating me like an invalid."

"I do think you should see a doctor. I kicked you with all my might. I thought you were some kind of crazed freak when you grabbed me."

"You were spying," he said, "I had a right to throw a little excitement into the mix."

"Well, you certainly did that."

Archer painfully gained his feet. "You have a very unusual accent that I can't place. And sometime, when there aren't birds singing in my head, you'll have to tell me how you learned to toss a big man like that. But right now, I'm moving toward my warm bed."

"I would say I'm sorry, but you really shouldn't have startled me."

"To think I worried about you, too," Archer said, not about to admit he'd been out looking for her. "Did you want something specific when you were peering in the window, or has maiming me satisfied you temporarily?" He sighed dramatically. "I need a whiskey."

"Marvella gave me some of her special concoction," Clover offered.

Archer suddenly towered above her. "Marvella!"

She nodded.

"Didn't I tell you not to go over there?"

Clover bristled right before his eyes, just like Tonk

before she threw a low-down, scurvy hoof. "You can't order me around, Archer Jefferson. I do as I please. I can take care of myself."

"So I see," he said grumpily. "Now, you go over to Marvella's, get your things and come right over here with me. This side of the street is where girls like you belong."

"Girls like me?" She put her hands on her hips. "What kind of girl do you think I am?"

"Innocent. Travel-weary. Unused to the ways of the world. You came here without a room or any reservations of any kind. Clearly, you didn't have a plan. That's how nice girls end up on the wrong side of the street. Listen, I know what I'm talking about. Marvella preys on girls who have no plan."

She stared at him. "She said the *Jeffersons* preyed on girls without plans. In fact, she said you Jeffersons had impregnated one recently."

"*We* impregnated? No, believe me, that's not exactly what happened."

"But it's close to true?"

He took a second look at Clover. She sounded so hopeful, as if she wanted to believe he was some kind of big bad wolf. Maybe he was, but not for this girl. She was not the type of girl he'd jump on in the woods as she traveled to grandma's. He liked his women spicy. If he had a dream woman, she'd be just the opposite of this lady. "You're very safe with me," he assured her.

He thought she looked doubtful, or maybe puzzled, so he realized this point needed to be outlined in teacher-red ink. "Do I *look* like the kind of man who feasts on innocent girls who can't see very well?"

Just then Bandera opened the door, peering out at them. "What's happening, friends?"

"Nothing. What are you doing up?"

"Can't sleep. Keep waking up, thinking about that lady on the bar stool. Think I'll go try to round her up."

Archer thought Clover gasped, but when he glanced at her, she was looking at her feet. Maybe a bug had crawled across her shoe. He figured her for the kind of girl who spooked easily. "Good luck," he said to Bandera.

"Whatever," Bandera answered. "I'm off."

His brother loped away. Archer met Clover's gaze. "So, *do* I look like the kind of man who preys on perfectly nice girls with strange accents? I'm trying to help you, traveler."

Clover didn't reply for a moment. Then she sighed. "Hope you feel better soon. I'm going to bed."

He watched as she walked away. What had that been about?

"Hey," he said, catching up to her in the middle of the street. Turning her to where he could see her in the bright lights from Marvella's, he said, "Don't go off mad. You kicked me, remember?"

"Yes. But harder than I meant to. Clearly I put you out of commission."

"Well, for a moment or two, but…" He looked at her, trying to see her eyes behind the thick lenses. "I mean, you didn't damage me for *life*."

She shook her head. "It's probably like a party balloon. Once popped, the air is gone."

He straightened. "Sister, there is *nothing* wrong with my party balloon! I am the *life* of the party when I want to be. That's *when* I want to be, and I just don't want to be. With…you know…you."

She looked at him. "Why not?"

He wasn't sure he heard her right. "Are you propositioning me?"

"I might be." She put her hands on her hips and a mulish expression on her face. "Scared?"

"Well, I'm not sure." He rubbed his chin. "It's just that you don't strike me as the kind of girl for casual charades."

"Well, maybe I am." She turned toward Marvella's. "You're not allowed to come in here unless you're a client," she said. "Good night, Archer."

There was definitely air in his party balloon, Archer realized. He liked her straightforward approach. "Wait a minute," he said. "Let's talk about this some more."

"No, thank you," she said. "I've discovered you're full of nothing but hot air, and I want a man who can have fun and then go home after the party is over."

"Isn't that supposed to be my line? I want a woman who goes home after the party?"

"If you had known your lines," Clover said, "you'd be getting a party favor right now. Good night."

She closed the door in his face.

His jaw dropped.

That crazy girl! She'd kicked him. She'd made his wounded soldier rise to the battlefield with all that talk about sex—sex with her—and then she'd shut the door on him.

The only door in town he shouldn't touch.

"DAMN," BANDERA SAID a couple seconds later, walking out the door to find his brother still standing there, hands on hips.

"Damn is right," Archer agreed. "What did Clover do once she went inside?"

Bandera laughed. "She went upstairs. You don't have the hots for her, do you?"

"No. I just hate to see a nice girl like her staying in a place like this."

Bandera shrugged. "She seems pretty confident."

"She does not! She needs direction."

"Dude, are you ever ignorant." Bandera stared up at the windows. "Never tell a woman she needs direction. You'll get a swift kick."

"I know." Archer sighed. "I already did, and strangely, I found it compelling."

"I can't worry about your love life."

"It has nothing to do with love. Merely concern for a stranger in town."

"That's what I'm concerned about, too."

"Your bar-stool lady not interested?"

"Not available," Bandera said. "She's not cutting hair or taking customers, according to the receptionist."

"Interesting. And too bad, as well."

"Yeah. Not too many women take a man's breath away like that one."

"Yeah." But Archer was still worrying about Clover. "That crazy Clover girl doesn't belong here. She should be at Delilah's."

"You may have figured her wrong," Bandera said. "She might be the kind of lady who can take care of herself."

"Yeah. I guess. Okay, I should git then."

Clover's exit to Marvella's still didn't seem right.

"Well, come on, then," Bandera said impatiently. "We don't need to hold down the porch all night."

"I know." Archer frowned.

"Look, if she puts the sizzle on your griddle, then go inside and talk to her. But if you're just being misguided and friendly, forget about it and let's get some shut-eye. She's fine."

"I think she wanted to sleep with me," Archer said.

Bandera laughed. "That shy, quiet girl? Nah. Besides, she's not your type."

"I changed my mind. I don't have *a* type," Archer said. "I have many types, as long as they don't come looking for a ring."

"You misread her," Bandera said. "Remember how we used to say that there were girls for fun, and girls for nun? That one would give you none, bro."

"I don't want anything from her," Archer said, turning to walk toward the Lonely Hearts Salon. "She has an attitude reminiscent of Tonk."

"And we call Tonk dog-faced. Think it over, bro."

"Clover's not unattractive," Archer said. He realized what Bandera had said. "And neither is Tonk!"

His brother laughed. "I pick the girl on the bar stool," he said. "I like a lady who's easy on the eyes."

"Looks aren't everything," Archer said stubbornly.

"But they are the first ticket to my heart, followed by my stomach being fed, my muscles being admired, my laundry being done, and my sex—"

"That's enough," Archer interrupted, getting crosser by the moment. "Glandular responses will remain undiscussed."

A window opened above them. "Archer!"

"What?" He wondered what his glasses-wearing newcomer wanted now.

"Where's the best place in town for drinks and dancing?"

Archer blinked. "Two-Bits."

"Thanks." She shut the window.

Bandera slapped him heartily on the back. "And you were worried about her being lonely. Sad. Homesick. A tragic heroine in a black governess dress right out of *Jane Eyre.*"

Archer turned toward Delilah's. "I can't picture Clover dancing." He didn't want to, either.

"It's the quiet ones who'll surprise you."

Archer shook his head. "I reckon."

"Night's still young," Bandera said. "If the wild girls are going dancing, maybe we should provide some partners."

"Now, that idea has some merit," Archer said cheerfully. He'd be willing to bet Clover's idea of dancing was standing by a plastic banana tree, watching everybody else shake a leg.

Finding out that she was an unwatered wallflower would make him feel a whole lot better.

Chapter Four

Clove realized there was a problem with The Plan after spending the early part of the evening getting to know Archer better. Though his e-mail conversations had been Texas tall tale, in person he was Texas short story, she thought, annoyed. All bark, definitely no bite. Not even a nibble.

Apparently, the hook was not properly baited. Bandera had really gone for her as the bar-stool babe. If Archer had, he'd tried to conceal it.

He concealed a lot, this cowboy she'd come to romance. Somewhat rude at times, and definitely in need of a manners injection. Not as kind and poetic as he'd been in cyberspace.

She felt a bit betrayed. He was not going to ravish her; in fact, she doubted he'd ravish any woman. He was more a chauvinistic protector. How dare he tell her she couldn't stay at Marvella's! Breathing deeply to get past the memory of his pigheadedness, Clove told herself to remember the bundles of babies his family had produced. Twelve brothers, for starters, and miscellaneous progeny.

"I just want one," she said longingly. "One."

John Wayne had had his good side, mixed in with his arrogance, she remembered. Still, Archer seemed to be more arrogant than cowboy gentleman.

"Well, at least my heart won't be in jeopardy where he's concerned," she told herself. A good stuntwoman always saw to her safety first, and after getting to know Archer better, she knew her heart was totally, completely safe.

"Maybe safer than I want it to be." She gazed in the mirror. When she'd yelled down to ask him about a place to go dancing, she had hoped he would offer to escort her.

He hadn't—and she had to admit that this cowboy was going to be tough to catch. The most bothersome part was that Archer wasn't remotely attracted to her.

Picking up a curling iron, she absently pressed a curl into her hair. It bounced when she released it—and The Plan took on a modification. She began to do her hair the way Marvella's girls had styled it earlier, Texas big and poufy. Tousled. Sexy. She applied the makeup the way they'd had it earlier, and then she shimmied into a tube-top dress she found in the closet. High heels completed her outfit.

"The revenge of the nerdy girl," she told herself, laying her glasses on the cosmetics tray. "Revenge is supposed to be so sweet."

The girls knocked on her door. "Ready?" they called. "Going out with us, Clover?"

"I'm ready!" Fluffing her hair one last time, she saw

the woman Bandera had admired gazing back at her. "I'm definitely going to Marvella's school to learn Hot-Babe Style 101. Then I'm going to get my cowboy," she said with satisfaction to her reflection. "Archer Jefferson, you're not going to know what hit you!"

"THERE SHE IS!" Bandera said as they walked inside Two-Bits bar. "The bar-stool babe!"

Archer peered through the smoky atmosphere and clinging partners. In the light from a neon beer sign, he saw her moving, laughing and snapping her fingers. Dressed in a dress practically painted on her lush body, she danced in a circle with a group of men and Marvella's stylists. "They're having fun," Archer observed.

"They sure are, and I'm on my way to do the same." Bandera took off to include himself in the circle, perilously close to the woman he fancied.

She was hot, Archer conceded. He liked a full-figured lady, and especially one with such nice skin. The breasts were nothing to ignore as they lightly jiggled under the tight material. Idly, he wondered if she was wearing a bra. Strapless dresses just begged to be tugged right off a woman, in his opinion. She had nice legs, and to be honest, he was a madman for high heels.

Checking the door, he wondered when Clover would arrive. He intended to keep an eye on her, because heaven only knew she could get in trouble in a place like this.

"You should dance with me," Bandera's beauty said.

He stared at her, then glanced at his brother. Bandera

was surrounded by three Never Lonely Cut-n-Gurls, and the evening looked to be going strong from his perspective. Bandera wasn't even glancing their way.

"I'm waiting on someone," he said.

She looked so disappointed, almost crushed. His bravado, which Clover and Tonk seemed to have teamed up to kick to smithereens, rose a bit.

"Now, don't take it too hard," he said. "You're beautiful, no question. I would dance with you anywhere, anytime."

"But?" she prompted.

"But I'm waiting on this crazy little girl to show up. She's new to town and real unsophisticated. You know what I mean? The kind who'd get lost on a sunny day."

Her eyebrows rose. She had clear, pretty blue eyes, and the just-teased tangle of her silvery-blond hair was appealing. Made a man's fingers want to wander there.

He glanced toward the door again. "She probably got lost on her way here," he said. "I should have offered to escort her."

"That would have been chivalrous," she agreed, "but you didn't, and so now you and I are stuck waiting for a mystery person to show up." She pulled him by the hand, though he didn't fight too hard. Once on the dance floor, he'd shift her over to Bandera, and go back to watching out for Clover. He shot a quick glance toward the potted banana tree strung with white lights, to make certain she wasn't hiding over there.

Cool skin slid into his arms, and he was jerked into the present predicament. "Gosh," he said. "You feel good."

"So do you, cowboy." She smiled at him, happy that she'd managed to disguise her accent completely.

They moved well together, Archer acknowledged. Bandera was glowering at him, but Archer shrugged. It had been ages since he'd held a soft woman, and this one was firm and ripe, and her lips were glossy—

"Once upon a time I dreamed of a cowboy like you," she said. "He was strong and powerful, and he knew how to romance a woman."

"I know how to romance a woman," Archer said. He could feel his arms warming from the heat her body was beginning to give off. Glowing embers turning to a sexual fire he hadn't felt in a long time—maybe ever. Frowning, he stared down at her, wondering if she knew she was working over his testosterone.

"You could show me," she suggested. "I like romance."

She was definitely coming on to him.

He glanced toward the door, watching for Clover.

The woman in his arms pressed lightly into his body, a full-length hint of the wonders available.

Taking a deep breath, Archer decided that opportunity only dropped sporadically into a man's life, and when it did, it needed to be seized by the throat.

"Think my brother had his eye on you," he said gruffly, his energy now captured by the fantasy of tugging the dress off of her.

"He may have," she said lightly, "but he doesn't know me like you do."

"Really?"

She looked at him with guileless eyes. Then she lowered her head onto his chest, in a gesture he would have to call gentle surrender. "Really," he heard her murmur.

That was it. Female-led seduction, his favorite pastime. He dragged her off by the hand.

CLOVE HELD HER BREATH as Archer led her to his truck. She got in when he held the door open for her, and then she stared out the passenger-side window, hoping he wouldn't look beneath the hair and curls to find plain ol' Clove. Unsophisticated, he'd called her. Thought he had to watch out for her, a touch of pity in his voice.

His hand snaked around her wrist, surprising her as he pulled her across the bench seat toward him. Then he kissed her hot and fast and hard, and in that moment, Clove knew she'd underestimated her man.

He was everything he'd bragged about in his e-mails.

He just wasn't showing it to "Clover."

The way she was now brought out the beast in him. She had rattled the cage.

Pulling back to look at her, Archer said, "Are you okay?"

She nodded.

"You went quiet on me."

It was too quiet in his truck. In the bar, it had been loud and they hadn't talked enough for him to recognize her. He'd also been scoping the door, not paying attention to her until she'd fairly propositioned him.

Switching the radio on to turn his mind from chivalry, she kissed him, reminding him of why they were in the truck.

"All right, then," he said a moment later. "I take it that means yes. I'm in the mood for a swim. Hope you are, too."

In February? Not likely, but if it meant getting him down to his boxers, then she would swim with polar bears in the Arctic.

He put his hand around hers, driving with his other hand. Clove closed her eyes, thinking about Lucy.

Just one baby.

A few minutes later, Archer parked the truck at a creek wooded with trees. He shone the headlights of the truck into the darkness for a few moments, then switched them to low. Putting the radio on a sexy jazz station, he said, "Now let's dance properly."

She went out the driver's side behind him, sliding into his arms.

"God, I never realized a woman could feel this good," he said. "You're like satin."

They danced together wordlessly after that, until the station went to commercial. Then he took Clove by the hand, leading her toward the water. "I was teasing about swimming," he said.

"I'm brave," she said softly. "I can handle it if you can."

"Skinny-dipping in February? No, my plan is to keep you warm."

She thought he would find a grassy spot for them to lie, but instead he walked with her, their fingers interlaced.

"This is one of my favorite places on earth. My brothers and I used to come here to swim after rodeos."

He ran a hand across her bare shoulders. Clove shivered at the caress, her breath held nervously.

"You're cold," he said. "Come back to the truck."

She wasn't cold, but she followed him, anyway, enjoying his concern for her. He let down the gate of the truck bed, spreading a blanket for them. Turning off the truck lights, he crawled into the bed, pulling her up to join him. Then he covered them with another blanket and rested her head on his chest.

"You're prepared for everything," she whispered.

"No, I'm not. If I was, I'd have a bottle of champagne cooling in an ice chest," he said. "See those stars?"

"Mmm," she said, loving the feel of his chest and hearing his heart beat fast.

"One of those stars has your name on it," he said. "What is the name of that star?"

"It's a secret," she whispered into his ear, straddling him to kiss his face.

"I like secrets," he said, pushing his hands underneath her dress to run his hands over her bare bottom. "You have on no underwear," he said with surprise. "You little daredevil!"

THERE WERE SECRETS and then there were secrets, Clove thought, quietly getting down out of the truck three hours later. She knew the town wasn't far, and she wanted to be long gone before her cowboy awakened.

It had been a night she'd never forget. They'd made the truck rock like mad, and she'd learned that giving up one's virginity was easy when the pleasure was that intense. They'd made love over and over again, hungry for each other. When he'd asked about birth control and offered a condom, she'd said she was fine.

At the final second, she'd confessed her virginity, hoping he wouldn't hop out of the truck.

He hadn't. He'd been quite tender and considerate of her.

She hurried, knowing Archer could wake up any minute and realize she'd left. It was a good thing she knew the real Archer, the grouchy one, or she would definitely have lost her heart to him tonight. What a tender lover! So romantic, yet so masterful. She got chill bumps thinking about it.

Thirty minutes later, she quietly let herself into her bedroom, closing the door. She took a shower, glad to be rid of the curls and the makeup. Snuggling into her covers, she smiled, thinking about Archer.

It was good to be herself again.

Only, tonight he'd changed her, made her feel beautiful. Given her appreciation of her woman's body.

She would never forget him.

Chapter Five

Three months later

In Delilah's kitchen, Clove straightened, her back sore. Cooking at Delilah's was nice, especially because Delilah was so kind. So was Jerry, Delilah's trucker boyfriend. Delilah hadn't really needed another employee, but the fact that Clove was only in town for a short while, until her visa ran out, was a plus.

Clove didn't really need a job, but she wanted to keep busy and make friends. All the ladies at the Lonely Hearts Salon were very eager to make her feel at home. In fact, she liked it here much better than at Marvella's, as Archer had said she would.

Marvella had been nice to her, but Clove had begun to feel uneasy about the male clientele who came to the salon.

"Triplets," the young, pretty doctor had told her at the last appointment. "Congratulations. You hit the jackpot! The first triplets ever to be born in Lonely Hearts Station, I do believe."

Clove had staggered out of the doctor's office, and she was still reeling. Triplets! She might have known that Archer Jefferson was capable of not only impregnating a woman, but doing it in an embarrassingly huge way!

She'd moved out of Marvella's the second she got home from the doctor's office, telling Marvella she felt she'd overstayed her welcome. The truth was, if Archer had felt strongly about Clove not staying at Marvella's when he barely knew her, she knew he'd really freak if he ever accidentally found out his progeny was gestating there.

"I've really done it now," Clove told Delilah, who was putting some plastic wrap over peanut-butter cookies Clove had baked.

"Don't worry," Delilah told her. "You're among friends here."

She was, but for the first time in her life, she was frightened.

"Have you thought of telling the father?" Delilah asked.

Archer had said, on many occasions, he didn't want children. "He wouldn't be happy. I'm skipping that conversation for now."

Besides which, she was already gaining weight. Her face was puffy and her breasts had swelled. If he'd thought her plain and unsophisticated before, now she was downright, well, more plain.

"The thing is," she told Delilah, "triplets are intimidating."

"You'd better believe it," Delilah said. "Pregnancy can be intimidating. You're doing it times three." She looked at her kindly. "If you ever want to talk about the father, you can trust me to be silent."

Clove lowered her eyes. "I'm afraid you'd be surprised. It's not anything I can share. But thank you."

Delilah nodded. "I'm going to my room now." She patted her hand. "Have a cookie and a cup of hot blackberry tea. Go to bed soon, too."

Clove smiled at the older woman. "Thank you so much. For everything."

Delilah smiled and left the room. Clove sat at the table, with only the lamp lit, rubbing her stomach absently. She wore dresses now, with expanding waistlines. Normally, a pregnancy wouldn't show at this juncture, but her three babies seemed to be thriving.

If they were destined to be Archer's size, she was in for a rocky road. She felt as if she was in the middle of going down a slide, and couldn't stop, no matter how much she wanted to. There was no body double who could perform this stunt for her.

Sighing, she pushed her oversize glasses up on her nose.

"Hey," a masculine voice said suddenly, making her gasp with fright. "What are you doing here, Clover?"

She stood, her heart pounding, her gaze drinking in Archer as he walked into the kitchen. She'd managed to avoid him while staying at Marvella's. She should have known she couldn't hide from him now that she was at the Lonely Hearts Salon. "What are *you* doing here?"

"Looking for cookies and milk. Came in the back way, as I always do, and a pit stop in the kitchen before bed is a necessity." He glanced at the cookies on the tray in front of her, then his gaze caught on her stomach. She watched with some horror as his attention traveled to her swelled breasts, then back to her stomach.

His eyes wide, he met her gaze.

"Oh, you poor thing," he said. "If you want me to kill the jerk, I swear I'll bring an army of Jeffersons down on his head. He'll wish he'd *never* done you this way."

"Archer," she began uncomfortably. "I'm all right."

"You're not all right," he said. "If you were, you wouldn't be unmarried, pregnant and living in a salon."

She swallowed. "I wasn't seduced and then left, if that's what you're thinking."

He looked at her doubtfully. "Clover, listen. You're a nice girl. Very trusting. But that's just what a man can be capable of. Making a woman love him and then leaving her."

She blinked. "It was the other way around. Not that you love me, but…"

He looked at her funny for a moment, as if someone had told a bad joke he didn't get. A muscle near his eye twitched. Slowly, his hand unsteady, he reached to pull her glasses from her face. He pulled her ponytail down, his fingers trembling.

She sensed him pulling away from her.

"Oh my God," he murmured. "Oh, no."

Clove's heart sank.

"This can't be," Archer said. "You can't be her. You can't be pregnant." To say that he was horrified would be putting it mildly. She could see in his face that he still didn't want to be a father. He was not in love with her. In fact, he hadn't known she was who she was. "Tell me I'm dreaming," he said. "A big, huge, ugly nightmare."

She blinked at his harshness.

"I'm sorry," he said. "I mean, we went looking for you that night at Two-Bits. Well, Bandera was trolling for the bar-stool babe, and he took off with three stylists he met dancing that night. I was hanging around waiting for you to show up, thinking you needed a guardian eye. But *you* were the bar-stool babe." He frowned. "I really thought you might need my protection."

"I was fine."

"That's what you said that night when I asked you about birth control." Archer told himself his heart wasn't going to bust a valve; taking a deep breath, he made himself calm down. "You said you were *fine*."

She sank into a chair. "I was fine."

"Not if you're pregnant!" he yelled. "Clover, that is not the definition of *fine!*"

They stared at each other.

Archer couldn't believe his bad luck. One more Jefferson to add to the mix of booties and diapers at the ranch. Mason was going to explode. Hell, *he* was going to explode.

"I suppose you want me to marry you. That's what you're hanging around Lonely Hearts Station for."

"No." She shook her head. "I'm hanging around because I didn't expect to get pregnant this fast, and my plane ticket isn't for another two weeks."

His eyes went wide. "This fast? You didn't expect it this fast?"

"Yes. I have a four-month visa from Australia."

"Australia?"

"Yes," she said softly. "TexasArcher, I'm Clove Penmire. AussieClove, from Down Under."

"AussieClove," he repeated stupidly. "No wonder you haven't been answering my e-mails. You've been here."

"Yes."

"You came here to meet me."

She nodded.

He thought hard, realizing by her tame responses that he was digging to the bottom of a very deep well. "You came here to get pregnant by me."

"I hoped so."

"You came here to marry an American."

"No. That was never my intention."

"So you just wanted a baby?"

"Yes." She looked away for a moment, then met his gaze defiantly. "Only The Plan went a bit awry."

"I'll say," he said bitterly.

"I'm having three."

The world seemed to drop away from his feet. He stared at her, his gaze narrowed. *"What?"*

She never flinched. "I'm having three babies."

Archer's ears rang, his stomach pitched, his eyes burned. Anger made his body tighten, his guts a pinched cord of disbelief. "Congratulations," he finally said, stalking from the room.

He stood in the hall, gasping for breath, waiting for

the stars of fury to leave his vision. AussieClove the stuntwoman had come here to get pregnant by him. The babe at Marvella's and plain ol' Clover were the same person. Whoa. She'd laid a trap and he'd fallen into it like a dope. Amazing what makeup and some curls and high heels could do to turn a man's brain to mush!

This made no sense, though. After their night together, she'd made no effort to contact him, not even under the AussieClove e-mail address—and he would never have put two and two together—so was she done with him? It sure appeared that way. He reached for the one thing he could fight about, even if it wasn't likely.

He stalked back into the room. "This is about money."

She glared at him. "Could you step one foot closer, please, so I can slap you? I really don't want to chase you to do it, because you're not worth it."

"I'm not worth it? Who is the brain behind the lying, cheating plan, Clover? *Clove?*"

"Do you want these cookies or not? I'm going to put them away." She picked up the tray of assorted cookies, tightened the plastic, and put them next to the coffeepot for visitors to find. "I've been baking all day, and now I'm going to bed."

"You're staying here?"

"Yes, I am." She moved past him, and Archer itched to grab her and make her stop bustling around as if his world hadn't come to a bull-stomped halt. He followed her down the hall. "When did that change?"

"When I found out I was pregnant. I moved over

here. Because you had wanted me at Delilah's in the first place."

She went up the stairs, and he followed her, carefully avoiding watching her fanny, though it was a herculean effort. "You got pregnant, and *then* you started taking my advice?"

"Yes."

Nothing about this moment made any sense. "Maybe I should find a stud for Tonk. If all a woman needs to mind is to become preg—"

She whirled on the stairs in front of him. "I didn't take your advice so much as make a decision for the good of my children. Cool it with the cowboy macho, Archer."

"Now just a minute." He followed her into her bedroom. "I am macho. I am somewhat chauvinistic, hard-headed and generally not a role model for young children. You knew all this. And still you came all the way to Texas to get pregnant by me."

She jerked a nightgown from a drawer. "Yes, I did."

"Aren't there any real men in Australia?"

"Plenty. But you were less complicated. Plus, you bragged all the time about your potency and it was just too tempting. Excuse me."

He sank into a chair as she went into the connecting bathroom and closed the door. "Triplets, damn it. Triplets!"

"Okay, so you weren't bragging," she said through the bathroom door. "Give yourself a gold medal." She came out of the bathroom in a white nightgown that went to her neck, touched her wrists with lace, and hovered at her ankles with more frothy lace. It billowed about her body, leaving everything to the imagination.

"Jeez," he said with some horror. "You're either trying to be a frilly ghost or a gothic heroine. Where's your candle and lantern?"

"The nightgown's practical, it's expandable for three, and it's modest enough for a home like this. So sorry it's not your idea of sexy."

"I'll say." He gulped.

She turned off the light. "Shut the door on your way out, please."

Man, she was a bossy one. She might not like being compared to Tonk, but his Appaloosa and his Australian had some mighty tight tempers on them. It made him want to jerk on the reins hard, but what he'd learned was that the more attitude a woman gave him, the softer his hands had to be.

"Hey." He reached over, switching the lamp back on. "Betty Crocker, you're going to be a little late for your baking tomorrow. We've got to talk this out."

She sighed and shoved a pillow behind her back so that she was sitting up. "I think we should not talk ever again."

"I'm confused."

"That's your problem."

"Maybe, but it would be best for the children if we talked." The three children, he thought, his heart pounding with fear.

A scratching in the hall made Clove jump from the

bed in a billow of white and fling open the door. She scooped a cat from the floor, closed the door and got back into the white-sheeted bed. "The four children."

"Four?"

She smiled. "Four children. This is my new baby, Tink." The gray-and-white cat observed him from its secure place in Clove's lap, its large, clear-water green eyes seeming to laugh at his plight. "I named her Tink after Tonk. Because she's tricky like your Appaloosa. Plus, she has lots of spots, just like Tonk. Of course, she doesn't have spotted nostrils like Tonk, but—"

"Okay. Let's stick with human babies conceived by me," Archer said crossly. "Ones without bobbed tails."

"Oh," Clove said, sympathizing with her cat. "It's only half-bobbed. And she's still beautiful, in my eyes."

Archer glared at the feline. "I do not like cats."

"What man does?" She smiled at him. "Well, some do. Very secure men do."

"Pregnant women aren't supposed to have cats. They carry diseases," he opined majestically.

"And I can't take you back to Australia with me," she said to the purring cat. "But Delilah says she'll give you a good home once I'm gone."

"Back up," he said. "I think we overlooked something in the conversation. You're not going back to Australia."

"Yes, I am," Clove said. "I don't like it here. The air is all wrong, for one thing. It doesn't smell right. It sort of smells like an old train depot. And—"

"Which it is. Clove," he said, certain his brain was going to stroke out from his rising temper, "you are not taking my children to a continent affectionately called Down Under."

"You're suggesting that I take them to a ranch affectionately called Malfunction Junction? *That* sounds like it would be good for the children."

She was making him crazy with her defiance. Strangely, he couldn't stop thinking about the pleasure her body had made him feel, and all the sassing he was receiving was giving him a fair-size urge to one-up her with some silencing kisses.

"Anyway, it's not like you were completely innocent in this," she told him. "You told me I'd bent your baby-making delivery system. Ruined the pipes for good. Put the factory out of commission. How was I supposed to know you were better?"

He frowned at the memory of her kicking him. Funny how the sexual pleasure they'd shared had wiped out his memories of the first time she'd had him flat on his back, gasping for breath. "Hey!" He sat up suddenly. "You hurt me. You really hurt me!"

She blinked. "It's in the past, Archer. I really think that, since you got me pregnant with triplets, the factory was only on a fifteen-minute shutdown."

"But I may have overlooked a really bad sign. What if the Curse of the Broken Body Parts hit me?"

"No, I hit you." Clove shook her head. "I may have been cursing you, but you did scare me and—"

"You don't understand." He scratched his head, shoving his hat back. "You really kicked me *hard*."

"Yes, and still you managed to send three healthy

sperm to do their job." She glared at him. "Don't tell me you're a hypochondriac. That would be so unappealing."

She didn't understand. The Curse of the Broken Body Parts had hit all of his brothers—right before they got married. Everything was moving too fast. "I find it somewhat ironic and downright hilarious that you nearly kicked in the holy grail of your quest. You should be gentler around the goods, specifically if you've come twenty-four hours and bought an expensive plane ticket to enjoy them." He sighed. "I suppose you're going to want money eventually. Support payments."

"A hypochondriac and a chauvinist. And I crossed a big ocean to be with you." Clove sniffed disdainfully.

"You're a sperm-stealer wearing a Thanksgiving-dinner tablecloth," he said. "Looks like we're going to be the proud parents of triplets. Please put the cat on the floor. It's making me nervous."

She sighed. "Tink, off you go. Big strong cowboy is afraid of you."

"No, I just need someplace to lay my pounding head." Kicking off his boots and tossing his hat into the chair, he got up into the bed next to Clove. "We need to sleep on this and see if we still like each other in the morning."

"We don't like each other right now!"

He flipped off the bedside lamp. "I know. We've got a lot of hard work ahead of us. Right now, I've got to get over the migraine you've given me."

"You cannot sleep in my bed."

"I sure as hell am not leaving you, Miss Defiance. As

soon as I turn my back, you'd probably give me the slip. I am here to mess up your plan, Clove Penmire from Down Under. Consider us wearing golden handcuffs. Mmm," he said thoughtfully, "that actually sounds fun. Consider us wearing golden balls and chains, which are connected forever at the ankle. Awkward," he mused. "Make that one ball, two chains and three baby-size ankle weights."

"I get the picture," Clove said, annoyed. "You're not leaving."

"That's right. You invited me into your life by being so devious. And believe me, I know just how to handle devious."

She sighed and inched her pillow down next to his. But he could feel her hanging on to the edge of the bed, in order to keep as much room as possible between them.

"We're going to have to get a bigger bed," he said, "because I have a feeling you're going to get as big as a house. That voluminous nightgown is only a precursor of more awkward things to come."

"Archer!"

He closed his eyes. Black spots of tiredness danced behind his lids, reminding him of Tonk and the low-down, scurvy hoof she liked to throw every once in a while to keep him honest.

He'd be watching out for Clove's attempts to kick him when he wasn't looking—because the first kick she'd thrown had been breathtaking.

Chapter Six

Clove awakened early the next morning, shifted Archer off her back where he'd settled comfortably and took his hand out from underneath her gown, where, to her dismay, it had come to rest quite proprietorially on her stomach.

He slept like the dead, his face buried in her hair.

Having never had a man in her bed before, this presented a dilemma. She liked having him sleep with her. Too much. He was loud and ornery and thought he knew everything, but when he wasn't expounding opinions and his eyes were shut, he was quite pleasant. Warm. Strong. Sexy.

How could she be strict of will when she really admired his possessiveness toward his children?

She was just going to have to stick to the original plan, for Lucy's sake. In fact, she needed to call Lucy—right now. It was just about the right time in Australia to drop a major bombshell.

She left the sleeping cowboy, closing the door softly. Tink slept in Archer's upturned hat where he'd tossed it in the chair; the feline was curled up just as content- edly as Archer in Clove's bed.

Someone's fur was going to fly when Archer awak- ened to find his hat taken over—Clove didn't want to be around when he discovered Tink's newfound bed. Quietly moving down the hall, Clove went downstairs into the kitchen. Luckily there was no one there yet, as only Clove rose this early to begin baking.

She picked up the kitchen phone, placed the call, and the next sound she heard was Lucy's voice accept- ing the charges.

"Clove!" Lucy exclaimed. "I thought we'd hear from you sooner!"

"I'm sorry," Clove said. "I miss you. So much!"

"We miss you! How is your trip?"

"I'm enjoying it. Ready to come home, though. How are you?"

"Good, darling. Good."

"And Robert?"

There was silence for a moment. Then Lucy said, "Good as well. Everything is just fine."

Clove closed her eyes, hearing what Lucy didn't want her to know. "And the farm?"

"Well, the horses are good—miss you, of course— but we're still looking for the right situation to fix all."

Clove nodded. Taking a deep breath, she said, "I have a bit of news, actually."

"Do tell! I hope it's wonderful."

"It is. I'm pregnant."

"Pregnant!" Lucy gasped. "Clove! No wonder you haven't called. You met a man!"

"Well, he isn't the reason I haven't called. I should have called sooner, but—"

"But you've been having too much fun. I'm so happy for you."

"Well, truthfully, this isn't about fun. I'm not in love or anything." Strong like, maybe. Overwhelming attraction, admittedly. But love? Neither she nor Archer would claim that. "Neither one of us are in love."

"I guess your…the father knows?"

"Yes." Clove closed her eyes.

"And what does he say?"

He says a lot, Clove thought. *He says too much.* "He's still a bit shocked. I'm having triplets."

"Triplets!" Lucy gasped again, then started laughing with excitement. "Triplets! Please come home at once so I can shower you with love and affection and presents. I'll be an aunt!"

"Maybe more a mother," Clove said.

"Mother?" Lucy stopped laughing. *"Mother?"*

"I could use the help," Clove said. "It would be really hard for me to do stunt work and take care of three babies."

"You should stay home and take care of them," Lucy said.

"And pay bills with what?" Clove asked.

"Of course, we would help you—" Lucy began.

"Lucy, I do not want to be supported by my older sister. I don't want to be supported by anyone. And just think how much you'd enjoy having three little ones in the house."

"I would," Lucy said, her voice filled with longing. "It's a dream for me."

"And you really can't imagine me being as good a mother as you," Clove said. "The truth is, you're suited to be a mother, and I'm not. Oh, maybe for one, but three? It would be a disaster."

"I—I'll have to talk to Robert, naturally. He did mention adoption at one point, then sort of lost interest in that idea…and they are your children. Your angels. You would forever be the true mum. And I don't know about Robert, dear. He sort of…sort of loses interest in things these days."

Sort of losing interest in Lucy. Clove didn't have to hear the words to know them to be the worry on Lucy's mind. "It's okay, Lucy. I'll be home soon."

"I'll start decorating the nursery!" Lucy began sobbing. "Clove, this is wonderful, a dream come true. I mean, I hope you're happy. You're quite sure this man doesn't love you? I will be quite happy to come over there and exert sisterly pressure on him if you would like me to. He should know that you are not some alone-in-the-world girl he can take advantage of."

"He does not love me, and I do not love him," Clove said with authority. "Trust me on this. We both understand that it was a one-night thing." It wasn't worth mentioning that Archer was asleep in her bed right now, determined to throw a wrench into The Plan. He didn't understand. He couldn't understand. Lucy and Clove had been there for each other when there was no one else. The sisterly bond between them was stronger than everything. She wasn't about to let Lucy down. "I love you," she told her older sister.

"You can never love me as much as I love you," Lucy replied, just as she always did. "Call me if you need anything. I'll be right there."

"I will."

They said their goodbyes and then Clove hung up, her heart feeling lighter than it had in a long time. She closed her eyes and put a hand on her stomach. "You are the luckiest children in the world," she whispered. "You angels are going to have a beautiful mother, a physician father, a lovely home, and me devoted to your every smile, your every tear."

"Those angels will also have me," Archer interrupted.

Clove's eyes flew open. Archer walked into the kitchen, crossing his arms as he stared down at her. "Let's review the roll call. I think I heard some errors in the lineup."

Clove stared at him, her heart pounding.

"Let's see," he said, holding up a finger, "first there's the beautiful mother, which naturally is you."

She blinked.

"Then there's the physician father. I'm not a physician. I'm a cowboy, third generation, Texas-born. So one of us is confused. You never mentioned that those were not my children, so that leaves us with a gap in the family history. When did I become a doctor? And what's my specialty?"

Her throat closed. She couldn't speak.

"What is my little Aussie stuntwoman up to now?" He pulled her into his arms, giving her a deep kiss. "Just as good as I remembered the first time," he said when he pulled away.

"Don't," she said sharply, whirling away from him.

"We should kiss more often," he said, "since we're getting to know each other for the sake of the children."

"No, we shouldn't," she said, going to open a bag of flour.

"Clove." He turned her toward him, trying to take the flour from her. "If I understood what you were saying on the phone, the answer is no. You are not giving my children to your sister."

She tugged the flour proprietorially and it dropped to the floor, sending a great white pouf into the air. For a reason she would never understand, Clove burst into tears.

"Yegods," Archer said, "it's only flour, baby."

Wiping her eyes, she managed to get flour everywhere. "You don't understand."

"I understand you have flour on your face, and that you've got three buns in the oven. My recommendation is that you give this job up and come home to the ranch with me where you belong."

Hands on hips, she said, "Archer, I do not need to be rescued. Stop trying to ride in here and toss me over your saddle."

He sighed. "You're very confused. But we'll soon fix that." Gently, he wiped the flour from her face. To her surprise, Clove liked the feel of his fingers stroking her.

She stood very still, letting him touch her skin, telling herself it was just the flour he was after, but secretly impressed by his steadfastness despite her tears.

"Let's get back to whatever you're baking. Then you need to turn in your resignation to Delilah."

There was a vast difference between steadfast and stubborn. Clove turned away. "Grab the recipe for the snickerdoodles out of the recipe box. That's what Delilah wants for her guests. She has a family of three from Wichita coming in, and she says that their e-mail reservation indicated that the little boy has never had a snickerdoodle. Delilah has a questionnaire for her guests as to what their favorite foods and desserts are, which I think is awesome for customer service." She turned to face him. "And I'm not turning in my resignation, thank you. I'm more than happy here."

"Here," he said. "The recipe for snickerdoodles, whatever they may be."

Handing her the card, their fingers touched, startling her because she hadn't expected it. Her thoughts suddenly were elsewhere. "I wonder what they'll be," she murmured, looking up at Archer in wonder.

"What?"

She blushed. "The babies."

He smiled at her. "Boys, of course. Boys who will always have the benefits of eating snickerdoodles."

Her eyebrows raised. "You think so? That they'll be boys?"

"Sure. And boys need to grow up around their uncles. Excellent role models."

She turned away.

"Not that your sister wouldn't be a good role model," he said softly, turning her back toward him. "Clove, I remember the e-mail you sent me mentioning that your sister couldn't have children. I could feel your pain and worry."

Her gaze lowered, hiding her thoughts from him.

"I reread those e-mails while I was home," he told her.

"You kept them?"

"Every one. And it's clear to me what happened. You practically mapped it out in your notes to me. I was always talking about myself, and you talked a lot about your stunt work, but throughout our correspondence, there were hints about your concern for your sister. It was a pretty common theme. Are you sure there's not more wrong in her life than not being able to have children?"

She frowned at him, not liking his thought process. "They've tried for years to conceive. With her husband, Robert, being a doctor, they've had access to advanced knowledge and opportunities. It should have happened."

"Maybe some things don't happen for a reason."

"I refuse to accept that."

"Obviously." He looked at her. "Part of me is flattered that you spent the money on a plane ticket, gave up your virginity and thought I could get the job done for you."

She raised an eyebrow. "And the other part?"

"The other part of me is ticked that you've changed my life without me having a say in it."

"You weren't supposed to find out, and—"

"But I did." He took her chin in his fingers. "And

that means that Lucy, as much as I feel for her plight, is now going to have to figure out a different way to have children."

Clove jerked away from his hand. "No."

"Yes. Those children are mine, and they are staying in America." He smiled at her gently, running a hand down her arm. "We may even have to figure out a way to like each other. It would be in the children's best interests."

"You didn't want me, Archer," Clover said defiantly. "Not the first day, when I asked you to dinner. You weren't interested. The only way I got you into bed was through the Never Lonely Cut-n-Gurls total makeover. But you didn't want *me*."

"True," he said cheerfully, "and blast those Never Lonely Gurls. I told you they were trouble, warned you to stay away from them. But you didn't listen, and now look at the pickle you're in."

She gave him a sour look and began scooping flour into a dustpan. "I don't want you to like me just because I'm pregnant with your children."

He got down to help her. "It wasn't that I didn't want you. I was busy with Tonk when you asked me out. And I sort of sensed you were the kind of unsophisticated girl who would require a lot of time and effort. A needy type, if you will."

She gasped.

"And my intuition was proven correct," he continued, ignoring her outrage. "You have turned out to be quite needy, a veritable time sink."

Standing, she washed her hands. "You are despicable, and full of yourself. I never saw that in your e-mails. I always wondered why a man who supposedly had so much going for him was content to chat with a woman for two years without ever seeing her face. It seemed odd."

"I like my freedom," he said happily. "All us Jeffersons do. But you have now snared me, and you will have to deal with the consequences of marrying a cowboy."

All her breath went right out of Clove's chest. "You're crazy."

"Then we'll get along, my sweet stuntwoman. By the way, you have let your stunt-work employers know you won't be coming back to work? Far too dangerous a job for a new mother."

"I am not marrying you. I am not listening to you. I think you are insane. You owe me nothing, and I owe you nothing, and that's the way we're going to leave it. Now get out, before I return to Marvella's." She gave him a pointed stare. "Where I know I'll be safe from *you*."

"I don't think so," Archer said, "for a thousand reasons I could share with you, but for right now, it's enough to say that you've invited me into your life, AussieClove, and this father will be sticking very close to his offspring."

Chapter Seven

"Mason can I talk to you?" Archer asked, three hours after he'd left Clove to her baking. He'd figured it was best to give her some time to chew on what he'd had to say.

"Sure." Mason glanced up from the paperwork he was writing on. "What's up?"

"I'd like to talk to everybody, if you can round up just the boys for dinner tonight. I need some advice, and I'd like to do it privately."

Mason rose. "Tell Helga we're going to have a sit-down, then." Their housekeeper would need to prepare enough food. "Leave a note on the kitchen board for the boys that you'd like everybody present."

Archer nodded. "Thanks."

"Are you all right?"

"I'm fine. I just need to air some things out. Need some guidance." He smiled, but it was tense. "Had a bit of a surprise today, and a family consult's the way I'd like to bring it up."

One thing was for certain, he was going about this differently than Last had. He felt Last had waited too long to talk to Mason about his baby. He'd avoided the problem. A man, in Archer's opinion, faced everything with his eyes on the horns. Last was the youngest, of course, and he had a lot of baggage being the Family Philosophe. They'd relied on him over the years, when they'd had their wild stages, to be the family compass. No one had wanted to let the baby of the family, with his incisive opinions of what a family should be, down. Consequently, Archer felt Last was so burdened by their need for him to be the strong one that when he faltered, it was tough for him to face it. Last had changed a lot lately, though, and Archer was proud of the strides he was making. Last sure liked baby Annette, and he and Valentine had turned out to be pretty good at routing visitation hours.

But my goal is to do things my way.

Either way, it wasn't going to be easy.

MASON, BANDERA, LAST, Crockett and Archer gathered at the family table, their plates piled high with barbecued chicken, red beans and rice, rolls and steamed broccoli. Though Calhoun lived nearby, oftentimes he and Olivia ate with Minnie and Kenny and Barley as a family. Two or three times a week, they joined the brothers at the main ranch house, particularly on the weekends, when Helga wasn't as overburdened by their presence, Olivia said. Helga loved Kenny and Minnie, though, and always claimed meals were better when as much family was around as possible.

With time, the brothers had begun to appreciate their

housekeeper's genuine love for their family. Besides, they couldn't not love Helga after her daughter Kelly had married Fannin.

"Group's getting smaller," Mason observed.

"Yes, it was even smaller when you were gone so long," Last said.

Mason put down his roll. "Well, you didn't have any trouble enlarging the family tree in my absence."

The rest of the brothers groaned at the continuing warfare and focused on their food. It was, Archer decided, not one reason but many that the moodiness around the ranch was so pervasive.

"Not tonight," he said on a sigh. "We're going to have to leave our war drums silent and cogitate on the newest issue at hand. I need your advice and not to be given several refrains of grief."

"What's up?" Bandera asked.

"Well," Archer said slowly, "I, too, will be enlarging the family tree."

Every brother stopped what he was doing, whether in midbite or mid-dig to stare at him.

"Go on," Last said with obvious interest. "Don't leave us in suspense."

"I'm going to be a father," Archer said.

"You don't even have a girlfriend," Crockett said, dumbstruck. "Don't you have to have a female for that?"

"Apparently not," Bandera said. "Let him finish."

At the head of the table, Mason had turned into a concrete gargoyle, his mouth open, his roll dripping butter onto his plate and the tablecloth.

"I'm going to be a father," Archer repeated. "To triplets."

So loud a gasp went up from the brothers that it was amazing the plates didn't jump an inch from the *whoosh*. Mason leaped to his feet, tossing his roll to the table. It bounced on the floor, to the delight of the dog.

"That is the last straw! What is the matter with you dunderheads! I taught you the condom song. I put condoms in the stockings at Christmas! And all you do is fornicate and populate! Every last one of you is irresponsible, immature and careless about the ranch's future!"

The dog, fearing she was being yelled at, grabbed her treasure and exited the dining room in a blur.

"Hello," Mimi Cannady said, sticking her head around the corner. "Am I interrupting anything?"

"Yes!" Mason roared at their next-door neighbor, and the only woman he'd ever cared about, though he was Johnny-come-lately to figure it out.

If he'd *ever* figured it out, Archer thought. "Mason," Archer said sharply.

"Sorry." Mason sighed. "Mimi, please. Would you care to have a seat and join us?"

"I think not. I just stopped by to let you know that I am putting the ranch on the market next week."

Mason sank into his chair, staring at her.

"Hate to eat without you, Mimi," Bandera said. "Grab a plate. Join the Addams Family as we dine. Lurch is speechless, as you can see, so it might be a pleasant meal for a change."

"No, thanks. I've upset Mason's digestion, so I think I'll head on off. Bye, guys." She went around the corner, then poked her head around the door frame. "You know, it doesn't look the same with just you five sitting there." Her blue eyes were wide with sentimental tears. "We really had some good times," she said softly. "I wish my baby was going to get to grow up on the ranch the way I did. But I guess that was a unique childhood."

Mason stared at the doorway Mimi had left empty. He glanced around at his brothers, his throat working, his face distressed and somehow older. "Dammit to hell and back," he said, throwing his napkin onto the table. "This place is a freaking zoo. I'm going out."

He left the room in the opposite direction Mimi had gone.

"Excellent," Archer said. "So far everything is normal."

"Oh, yeah," Crockett said sarcastically. "I think that went very well. Every night should be so warm and cozy. Next thing you know, we'll have our own reality show, just like the Brady Bunch."

"That wasn't a reality show," Bandera pointed out. "And Helga really isn't like Alice, do you think?"

The brothers glared at him. Bandera looked at each of them, then picked up his fork and began to chew forlornly.

"So…back to your announcement," Last said with a grin. "Triplets, eh? I cede the trophy for family error to you, bro."

"Who is she?" Crockett asked. "Anyone we know?"

"Even I don't really know her," Archer said. "She's an Australian stuntwoman."

"Dang," Bandera said, his tone admiring. "Hang ten, brother!"

"We need a woman who can put a little juice back into this family," Crockett said. "She sounds fun! An Aussie stuntwoman bearing triplets! Does she have an accent? Does she say, 'G'day, mate'?"

"Jeez." Archer ran a hand through his hair. "She's not what I would classify as fun. She has a slight accent. She's never called me mate, and we don't even come close to being friends. As far as the stuntwoman thing goes, as exciting as it might be, I'm making her quit her job. Too dangerous."

"You're making her quit her job." Bandera chewed and thought about that. "How did she take that?"

"Very well for a first mention, I thought."

"Which means he talked, she ignored him or possibly laughed in his face, and he plans to revisit the subject. So, are you moving Down Under?" Last asked. He looked thoughtful. "And…when's the wedding date?"

His brothers stared at him. Uncomfortable tickling began along his neck and continued up over his skull. Archer cleared his throat nervously. "Too many questions to be answered tonight. Let's eat this grub."

Crockett's eyes were round. "You *are* marrying the mother of your triplets, aren't you? We Jeffersons are going to start getting a bad reputation if the seed doesn't stop getting scattered with such enthusiasm."

Last glared at Crockett. "I know you're referencing me, and, in case it's any of your business, which it isn't, Valentine isn't interested in marrying me. Nor am I interested in marrying her. What happened, happened. We're happy with our baby, and we've worked it out just fine."

"I guess I have to know, Archer, in the spirit of family history and precedent," Crockett said, "did the Curse of the Broken Body Parts factor in? Did she hurt you?"

"Yes and no," Archer said crossly. "She kicked me."

"Kicked you?" Last asked.

"In the family jewels," Archer elaborated.

They stared at him.

"And you *still* eked out triplets," Last said, his tone admiring. "Had she not disturbed the House of Archer, you could be expecting quads or quints!"

"I don't know if that qualifies for The Curse," Archer said. "I saw stars and maybe a galaxy far, far away. But nothing broke, although it certainly felt crippled at the time."

"I think that means you're safe," Last opined. "The Curse is a precursor to courtship the hard way, but clearly she didn't kick you as hard as you thought she did. Although there is probably a story," he added thoughtfully, "that we need to hear about how a lucky brother goes from receiving a kick in the zipper to unzipping *her* zipper. Even a stallion usually treads carefully around a filly with aim."

"Did you ask this woman to marry you?" Bandera wanted to know. "Did you give her an option?"

"He doesn't have to answer that," Crockett interrupted. "I agree with Archer—let's just eat."

"You don't want to hear about marrying mothers,

Crockett," Bandera said, "because you've got the hots for Valentine."

Everyone gawked at Crockett now that the secret was out. The silence was stiff and somehow heavy. Uncomfortable. Embarrassed. He pushed back his chair, tipping it over, and left the dining room.

Last vacated as well, throwing his napkin onto his plate with fervor.

Bandera shrugged, got up and left.

Archer blinked as he sat alone. "Congratulations, Archer," he said to himself. "So happy for you, Archer. Fatherhood will suit you, Archer. Aren't you the lucky dog, Archer?"

Leaning back in his chair, he closed his eyes. "It doesn't matter." He had his own ideas about family and responsibility, and now that tricky Miss Clove had shanghaied him into being a father, everything—most importantly, her—would go by his set of standards.

Three little boys. They would grow up to be just like his brothers and him. Jefferson males. Hardworking, hard-loving. Hardheaded.

Just like Clove.

One of them was going to have to bend, because he had no intention of ending up without his woman, like Mason, or having custodial arrangements, like Last.

Clove was due a compromise, and he was excellent at the skill of convincing.

"ARCHER," CLOVE SAID when he returned late that evening with flowers, "you do not need to romance me. I understand you have an ornery need to try to change my mind, but that just shows me you don't understand how important this is to me. There is not going to be a compromise."

He grinned at her, slow and sexy. "Yes, ma'am." Handing her the flowers, he sat at the kitchen table. "I looked forward to your cookies all day long."

She looked at him suspiciously.

"Did I mention I like the new curves on your figure?"

"Flattery isn't going to work." She put her glasses on and gave him a look of disdain. "You passed me up when I was wearing these."

"And any man would," he said reasonably. "I can't even see your pretty eyes. Why do you wear those things?"

"Because I can't see."

"Obviously, or the salesperson would never have sold them to you. Here, let me help you." He slid them from her face. "Now, the real you. You shouldn't hide behind those things."

Clove blinked. "Hide? *Hide?* I never hide. I'm a stuntwoman. I'm brave, no different than you when you're on a bull or a bronc or your Appaloosa."

"I knew we had something in common. Bravery," Archer said with satisfaction. "This isn't going to hurt as much as we think it will."

"What won't hurt?" Clove gave him another suspicious look as she placed a glass of milk in front of him. "I can't bear to see you eat cookies without milk, but I am not serving you, for the record. I'm only complementing my baking."

He grinned, making her heart flutter. "Thank you," he said. "Even if you're not serving me. The cookies are delicious, and it won't hurt much to fall in love with you."

"What?"

He shrugged. "We're going to have to, you know. For the sake of the children."

"We're going to have to fall in love?"

"Yes. These are the best chocolate-chip cookies I've ever eaten. Do you stand in this kitchen all day and bake these wonderful morsels?"

"Yes. It's the trade-off Delilah and I made. She wouldn't charge me, though I said I wanted to pay her. But she said no woman related to the Jeffersons ever owed her a dime. No matter how many times I try to explain that I'm not related to the Jeffersons, she seems to think I am."

"Delilah doesn't know I'm the father?"

"No. I haven't told anyone. Remember, I didn't want you to know."

"And that makes me quite wary of you, AussieClove. Secretive wasn't something I saw in your e-mail persona."

"Guess we were both in for some surprises."

"Yes." He sniffed a snickerdoodle, his face wreathed with pleasure. "Definitely worth the wait. So how did Delilah know you were related to me?"

"I told her that you recommended I stay here—and I am *not* related to you."

"We are related by baby, and I'll pay your bill while you're here, at least until I move you to the ranch. You don't have to stay on your feet all day."

She ground her teeth. "Back to the have-to-fall-in-love part, I don't think that's how it works."

"I've done a survey of my family, and between those who have a working relationship with the mother of their child, and those who have fallen in love, Cupid is definitely preferable." He looked at her. "You have your reasons for doing things, and I have mine. We should work together on this—for the sake of our children."

He sounded so smug she wanted to argue. Wanted to throw a wall of denial at him, maybe even a cookie jar.

She had a feeling he'd throw it right back and call it fun.

Chapter Eight

"I came here to find you, by the way," Archer said, eating his cookie and reaching for another. He settled himself comfortably into a kitchen chair.

"Well, here I am."

He grinned at her curt tone of voice. "No, I meant, before I knew you were pregnant yesterday. I had returned here to start hunting for you. I was going to start by asking over at the Never Lonely if you had left a forwarding address."

She used a spatula to move some cookies onto a baking sheet, then put it down to come stand in front of him. Manfully, he resisted the urge to sweep her into his lap and give her a Texas-size smooching, starting with her earlobes and ending up at her toes. He'd done a lot of thinking now that he'd gotten his predicament off his chest to his brothers, and he'd decided this new family was going to go all his way.

He was going to be an excellent father, just as Maverick had been to him and his brothers.

"Were you looking for the plain me or the dolled-up me you made love to?" she asked.

He winked. "Wouldn't you like to know. But I believe in leaving a woman guessing."

She looked so sweet and so forlorn standing there, hoping he'd say the right thing. Archer grinned. She thought she was a tough girl, but she was sweet as a snickerdoodle. Her half-tailed cat wound around her ankles, meowing for attention. Clove's hair was silvery and chin-length blond—recently cut. He liked the style on her. It brought out the blue in her eyes and gave her a well-cared-for look. "So who cut your hair?"

"Delilah."

He nodded. "I should have known. The style is simple and attractive. I like it better than the bar-stool-babe style you had before." He looked at her for a moment, his thoughts flying. "You're pretty," he finally said softly. "And pregnancy agrees with you."

"You're avoiding the question."

"No, I'm not." He stood, taking her gently by the arms, which sent Tink scurrying to the hallway. Lifting Clove, he sat her on top of the counter. "I was merely looking for Clover, Clove, any way you look. I told you, I don't have a type. I like ladies in general. And all the girls like me."

Her lips parted in astonishment. He laughed. "But if you won't serve me, then you must feed me."

"I will not." She drew back a bit, but her eyes were on him, watching. He noticed she didn't push him away or hop down from her perch.

"I wanted to find you," he said, breaking a cookie into quarters as he moved between her legs, "because I couldn't forget you. Eat." He put the cookie into her mouth. As she chewed, he kissed her fingertips.

She swallowed. "Yes, but—"

"You talk too much. That's your problem. We liked each other better when we wrote and didn't speak." He fed her another piece of cookie and kissed the inner crook of her arm. "You smell like homemade treats," he said. "I find that strangely erotic."

"I wouldn't be surprised by anything about you that's strange."

He laughed, putting another cookie into her mouth. "What do you expect from a cowboy? I like my woman in the kitchen." He kissed her palm. "I like my woman in the bedroom." He ran a hand under the skirt of her dress, pulling her toward him and nearly off the counter. "I'm going to like my woman in every room of the house. And outside the house, wherever I can get you."

He slid her onto his waist so that he could kiss her above the sweetheart neckline of her dress. Her legs stayed wrapped around him. Archer groaned. "You stay sexy like this, and I'm going to have to make love to you, little mama."

"And when I'm not sexy? When I get huge? And can't see my feet?"

"I'll suck your toes," he whispered. "I promise you'll always be able to feel those little piggies just fine."

That made her slide down from his waist. He didn't stop her.

They stared at each other for a long moment.

"It's not going to work," she said.

"Why not?"

"I know you're doing this for the children. And while I appreciate your feeling responsible, I don't want a man that way. I've always been independent."

"You need to come to the ranch. See the real me before you decide what you want. I've seen the real you. I've seen several real yous. Now it's your turn."

She moved away. "I don't want to."

"For the children, you should."

She began putting away cutlery in a drawer. "We can't make something out of nothing. And that's what it would be. I did this for Lucy, and in my mind, my motivation is clear. Maybe not right or pretty, but clear."

He sighed. "If you don't want to go to the ranch with me, then let's take a weekend away where we can talk."

"If you talk, I might give in. That's what you want." She turned to look into his eyes. "You don't know what it would be like to be childless. You wanted to be that way for always. My sister did not. She loves her husband and wants him to be happy. This is the closest to real motherhood she will ever have, Archer. I can't let you sway me, and even if I could, I would always know you did it because of your sense of masculine pride. You ignored me both before and after the Cut-n-Gurls fixed me up. Suddenly, my pregnancy has you beating your chest like a caveman. But since you went back and read our e-mails, surely you saw your desire to always stay single and footloose. I have no desire to change that."

He sat down. "I understand about your sister. I sympathize. And no, this wasn't how I saw my life. But I'd be a cold human being if my heart didn't warm to the thought of three little babies with my blood, my genes and maybe my mother's and father's characteristics."

She looked away.

"You want me around," he said. "You want your babies to know their father. There's nobody like me. I'm rough-and-ready and a little wild, but I know how to take care of the people I love. And I am the kind of man who will love his children."

"Lucy and Robert will," Clove said, her voice trembling and not so sure of itself.

"Only in the capacity of aunt and uncle. I'm sorry, Clove," he said. "You had a good game and you pulled a good stunt, but I'm no fool. My children stay here, and if I have to make it a legal issue, I will do that."

Her eyes widened. "There's no way you can!"

"I can. Marry me, stay here, and bear my children on Texas soil. I'll take very good care of you. But if you fight me on this, I won't lose. Mason has suggested that, given your orneriness, the only way to make you see the light is with a custodial lawsuit. However, that didn't work very well in Last's case. I prefer to do things without lawyers. Especially since you and I are well suited to each other." He smiled. "I can't forget the little woman who got me all fired up in my own truck bed."

"You can't treat me the way you do Tonk. You can't just badger me until I do your wishes."

"I'd rather go about this like rational adults. It would

be best for all if you quit acting like a savior for your sister and let us go about our business."

She gasped. "How dare you?"

"How dare you do what you've done? It's sneaky and wrong and quite possibly the most heartless thing I've ever known a woman to do. You and I are quickly going to get sideways on this matter—"

"We already are. Good night."

Clove left the kitchen. Archer watched her go, his lips flat and drawn. What a dilemma he'd gotten himself into! She was so stubborn and truculent, like a mule in a garden patch. Then she could be all sweetly melting in his arms, driving him mad thinking about her body. His babies inside her body.

He wished she'd let him romance her so that they could capture something real before the babies arrived. From the way they'd made love, he knew there could be something between them. She'd been so innocent that night that the memory of it made him want to cry. She'd turned his heart to jelly with her intent to give away his children. He deserved the chance to prove himself a good husband, a good father, a good lover.

Now all they were going to see of each other, he supposed, was their bad sides.

He heard her bedroom door close upstairs. His jaw tight, he shook his head.

She was his virgin. She was going to stay his.

He headed up the stairs.

Walking into her room, he planted himself on the floor. "I plan on you and I getting along, Clove. We simply have to. I know we're on opposite ends of a very long spectrum, but you can't take my children, and you can't leave Texas."

She didn't say anything. She sat silently on the edge of her bed, not looking at him.

He frowned. "Clove, I sincerely believe something good could happen between us if you'll let it. I know I'm willing to try."

When she didn't move, retort or flinch, he went over and bent down in front of her. "Clove?" She seemed suddenly so pale. Brushing her hair behind one of her ears, he stroked her cheek. "Just because you're silent doesn't mean you've suddenly decided to agree with me, does it?"

She met his gaze. What he saw there frightened him.

"I have cramps," she said.

"Cramps?" He puckered his forehead. "Like, stomach cramps from something you ate?"

"I think...cramps." Sweat broke out along her upper lip.

"I don't think you're supposed to do that." Archer dabbed away the sweat and felt her palm. Cold. She was frightened. "Do you want to lie down?"

"I don't think so." Her eyes widened as she gazed at him. "I'm scared."

"Okay. Let's put in a call to the doc." Pulling his cell phone from his pocket, he said, "You know the doc, right? Pretty little thing? Makes no time for us Jeffersons except medically speaking," he babbled. "Hello, Doctor," he said, running a hand over Clove's shoulders to comfort her. "You've been seeing Clove… Great Scott, did you tell me your last name, AussieClove?" he asked.

"Clove Penmire," she reminded him.

"Clove Penmire, soon to be Jefferson," he said, drawing a groan from Clove. "But we'll take care of the particulars later," he said hastily. "Clove mentioned she's cramping in her tummy. I don't think she's eaten much today, maybe a cookie or two, and we've been bickering a bit, though I don't think I upset her bad enough to cramp…oh, all right. We'll be right there."

He hung up. "Clove, the doctor says for you to come on, sweetie. Those were her words, not mine. I mean, she was saying it to you, not me—"

"You're rambling," Clove said. "Do you always do this when you get nervous? From your e-mail correspondence, you never struck me as excitable. I always thought you sounded so brave and devil-may-care."

"Well, whatever gave you that impression was wrong. I am brave, but right now, as the father of these triplets, I am exercising my right to ramble. Let's take these stairs slowly, sweetie."

"I wouldn't want you to lose your footing," she told him.

"No, you wouldn't. It would be an ugly sight, me rolling down the stairs, boots over head." He was rattling, and it was helping him feel better. Cramps! That didn't sound good. He didn't want anything to happen to Clove—or the pregnancy she'd come so far to conceive. "Maybe my sperm weren't as robust as I thought they were," he muttered.

"That's just as likely as me saying perhaps I shouldn't bake so many cookies."

He appreciated her attempt at humor because he'd broken out in a sweat. "The truth is, now that I know I'm going to be a father, I'd like to stay in my exciting position. I'm going to have three boys! Here, sit here," he said, helping her slide into his truck. "Calm down, everything is going to be just fine."

She gave him a glare. "Archer, I am calm."

"Oh. Okay." He ran around the vehicle, hopped inside, turned the engine and accidentally gunned it. "Sorry."

Her face was so pale. His fingers tightened on the wheel. "Everything's going to be fine," he repeated, more to reassure himself than her.

TWO HOURS LATER, Clove let Archer lead her from the doctor's office. She was tired, but mostly relieved.

And not surprised. "It would make sense that you and I have completely incompatible Rh factors."

"Isn't that odd? I never knew my blood type until today."

"As irresponsible as it seems, I didn't, either. I'm twenty-six, and I didn't even know there was such a thing as an Rh factor. And I'm one of the fifteen percent who is negative," Clove said.

"It seems the doc should have checked you for this before."

Clove sighed. "I didn't ask you your blood type, Archer. You would have spooked, I'm sure."

"I probably would have. No matter," he said cheerfully. "A little injection to your rump was the answer. I hope," he said, sounding worried again. "I mean, I know it's all good. And that crazy little doc even managed to get a blood donation out of me."

Clove giggled. "You looked so perplexed when she told you that big boys give blood quarterly." She glanced over at his bandaged arm. "You never told me you were afraid of the sight of blood."

"I'm not. I've seen plenty."

She outright laughed at his growl. "Everyone's but your own, I guess. Dr. Fern said she figured taking blood out of you would keep you from being so antsy for a while."

"In all this time, we have never known that doctor's name. Who would have ever thought that gorgeous doc's first name was Edna? My brothers are going to have heart failure. No one can marry a girl named Edna Fern!"

"She says she doesn't want to marry or even have a boyfriend. Dr. Fern says all the men around here convinced her that she's better off single for now. Patching them up and hearing them wail after rodeo injuries made her think she was better off with her cat, dog and bird. And I think she said she lives with her elderly grandma."

"Well, there you have it," Archer said. "No one will risk her wrath anymore by trying to ask her out. Luckily for me, I'm spoken for."

Clove knew he was teasing her, but at the same time, she didn't want to start feeling comfortable with him. "Did you ever try to ask her out?"

"Nah. She's too smart for me."

Clove gasped. "I'm very smart!"

He laughed. "And jealous, too. Glad you're feeling possessive of me."

She crossed her arms and looked out the window. "I hate the idea of being house-bound for the next few days."

"I think it sounds like fun. We're going to watch videos, read great literature… Did I ever tell you my father was a huge fan of Brit lit? We went to public school, but my parents were big on home—"

"Wait," Clove said. "*I'm* confined to bed. You're not."

"Where you are, I am. You have no family here, and it's up to me to take care of you. Lucy would want that," he said logically, clearly pleased with his argument.

"Archer, you are smug, self-assured, over-confident and—"

"And those were all the reasons why you bought a plane ticket, my dear. You wanted me, you got me. And you're going to love reading the paper in bed with me every morning. I'll read the financial section and the funnies, and you can have 'Hints from Heloise.'"

She had no reply for that. Part of her wanted him around because as loony as he was, he was fun, and he kept her mind off her problem. She'd been so frightened of miscarrying! The fear that had washed over her at the thought of losing these babies still sat inside her. They were becoming so real to her; her pregnancy was bringing her a joy she'd never expected.

Besides, being bed-bound with Archer was something many women would dream. The con was that they would get on each other's nerves; the pro was that she fully remembered how sexy and considerate he could be. They couldn't make love again, and probably never would, but he was outrageous company, something her daredevil heart enjoyed. Even when he was playing the irascible, wayward cowboy hunk.

Yet she could not allow him to take over her life the way he wanted to. He was bossy and stubborn. Even his horse rebelled.

"The only question left for us to answer, I guess is," Archer said, "my bed or yours?"

Chapter Nine

"Never mind," Archer said suddenly as he pulled up to Delilah's salon. "I don't think it's a good idea for you to walk upstairs. I'm thinking stairs are verboten. You stay here, and I'll go pack for you."

"No!" Clove moved to open the door.

He reached out and caught her fingers. "Clove, I know you want to rebel about everything, but stairs cannot be a good thing for a woman who's been given orders to rest. I will pack your things."

"You can't pack my things!"

Her eyes were so tired, he thought, though even the dark circles were attractive.

She made him want to protect her, he realized. For all her blowing in the wind about how independent she was, he knew she needed him. And that made her more attractive.

"I think I really like you," he said slowly. "I know you won't believe that, but you're doing something funny to my heart."

"I don't know why," Clove said.

"I don't, either, because heaven knows, all you do is rile me." He shook his head in wonder. "I'm pretty sure I was meant to have a brunette who likes to fish. Fishing is comfortable for the soul. I think she should like fishing, sex and pool."

"Fishing comes before sex?"

"Yeah, but only because I dream of making love in a boat, out in the middle of a lake, where no one is around, just me and my gal and the night sky overhead—"

She sighed. "In Australia, we would make love on an ocean."

"Yeah. I can see that," Archer said enthusiastically. "You see why fishing is so critical. After we make love, we'll have a finned creature or two to toss on the barbie." He winked. "Did you notice me trying to incorporate some Aussie slang?"

She wrinkled her nose. "You may call it that, pardner. I'm getting out of this truck now, and I'm going to giddyup to my bed, where I am staying till this storm blows over."

"Very nice on the slang part, but you're staying put, and I'm fetching."

"Is that slang?"

"It's fact," he said. "Don't move."

He got out of the truck. She slowly got out on her side.

"No, Clove," he said. "You have to stay here. No stairs. Dr. Fern did not okay you for stairs."

"I'm going to the top of the staircase, and then I won't come down for two weeks. That's my plan."

Gently, he helped her sit back down in her seat.

"Clove, I have a ranch to help run. I cannot leave you here alone. Those are my children, and I'm going to see to their safety and your well-being. Delilah can't take care of an invalid for two weeks. She has a business to run." He touched his fingers to her cheek. "It's time to say, 'Yes, Archer.'"

"That's what got me into this predicament," she told him.

"No, what got us into this predicament was me saying yes to you. You and I are still going to have a talk about that one day, because you pulled a Tonk on me, and if you weren't so much my kind of girl, I'd be madder than heck."

"Your kind of girl?" Her look of surprise caught at his heart.

"Yes. I think you must be. We had two years' worth of e-mail correspondence between us, and I know we both had separate reasons for writing, but I know I enjoyed having an Aussie pen pal, despite the fact my brothers thought I needed more in my life than a cybergal. I thought you were one of the most interesting women I'd ever talked to, and I have clearly been proven correct. But despite that, the saying goes that we must be careful of the seeds we sow. You sowed three seeds, and I'm going to harvest those little bundles of joy in about six months. Sit. I'll be right back."

She seemed to do as he asked, so he headed up the stairs. Of course, she was liable to disobey or disappear on him, so he had to pack fast. She'd come to town, he recalled, with one tiny suitcase, so he grabbed that from her closet and shoveled undies and other drawer contents into the suitcase.

He cleaned out her makeup drawer in the bathroom without hesitation. Grabbed shoes and clothes from the closet, cramming them into the suitcase. He wasn't doing a very good job, but they were only going to be in the case for about two hours. The bottle of perfume on the dresser, he figured, should go on top so it wouldn't break.

It was then that the picture on the mirror caught his eyes. Clove and another woman hugged each other, each laughing for the camera, clearly having the time of their lives. Turning the picture over, he read the inscription. "To the best sister in the world. The only one I trust and can run to at any time. If it wasn't for my brave sister, I wouldn't be alive today. There is no one like you, Clove. I love you. Lucy."

Frowning, he blinked, rereading the inscription. His heart hammered, felt as if it was knocking on a piece of his soul with a bad omen. Restless worry came over him as he read it a third time.

Then he quietly laid the photo in the suitcase, closing it tight.

ARCHER WAS QUIET on the drive to his ranch, so Clove fell asleep. When she awakened, he was listening to soft country music, his face was grim, and he was pulling into the driveway of a very large ranch.

"Wow," she said. "Did you mention in any of your e-mails to me that you lived on a real ranch?"

He frowned. "What do you mean?"

"I mean that this is beautiful, and seems to go on and on, except for that cute house on the hill."

"That's Mimi's house, at least for another week. She's selling out, which has my brother, Mason, in an uproar. Try to ignore him."

"All right." She got out and Archer came around to take her arm.

"How are you feeling?"

"I'm fine! Just tired." She pulled her arm away.

Several big men came out onto the front porch, waving at them. Archer took a deep breath. "Welcome to the family," he said. "The very diluted version."

She was nervous. They were obviously more nervous, which surprised her, because she wouldn't have expected such big men to be that way about anything.

"Clove," Archer said, "these are my brothers. Mason, Last, Bandera and Crockett. I have more, but they're sort of dispersed for the moment. Bros, this is Clove Penmire. You may recall that I had an Australian pen pal. This is she."

They solemnly shook her hand. Her face burned with embarrassment. Of course, they knew she was pregnant, she realized as they all slipped surreptitious glances at her stomach. Which meant they also knew that she had shanghaied Archer's sperm.

They had to think she was an opportunist and very likely after money. For the first time the result of her actions hit her. She'd been so busy thinking about Lucy, she hadn't considered Archer's brothers. If Archer had done what she had done, Lucy would be very angry and would probably never like him.

She put her head down.

"Welcome to the family," Mason said gruffly. "You need to get inside. Archer, can I talk to you privately?"

"Sure. Will you guys introduce Clove to Helga—our and Mimi's housekeeper—and if Calhoun's around, his gang, too. Help her get settled."

With a pang, she watched Mason and Archer walk away.

"Let me get your stuff," Last said kindly. "I'm sure you'd like something to eat, so let me show you to the kitchen. Helga always has something tasty sitting out for us. You fellows go on. I can handle settling Clove in."

They nodded to her, apparently happy to let Last be in charge of her, and moved away.

"Sometimes we talk a lot," Last said, "and sometimes we don't. Today we seem to be a taciturn bunch."

"I'm sure I'm unexpected," Clove said faintly.

"Yes, you are, but if you only knew how much happens around here that's unexpected, you wouldn't worry a bit. Besides, you'd be surprised at how much of our unexpected happenings turn out to be blessings."

She blushed. "I guess you know I'm expecting."

He grinned. "We may be taciturn, but we don't keep many secrets. Congratulations, by the way. We like babies around here."

"Oh, I won't be staying here," she said hurriedly. "After I get through with this period of rest, I must return to Australia."

He looked at her, settling his hat back on his head. "How about you don't owe me any explanations, and how about I find you a cookie and some tea in Helga's kitchen?" Gesturing for her to follow, he carried Clove's bag into the kitchen. "We didn't like Helga's cooking when she first came here, but now we consider it a good thing. Most especially when it's cold outside. She can cook a cabbage soup that would make you cry with joy, believe it or not. And her poppyseed cake will take your breath away."

She smiled at Helga, who gave her a broad wink.

"More babies," Helga said. "Good!"

Last chuckled. "We don't have secrets, as I said. Sit right here and let Helga fix you up. I'm going to head out for the moment, and figure out where you're sleeping tonight. We have three houses on the ranch, and we want you where you can rest comfortably."

"Thank you." Clove sat silently, appreciating the warm cup of steaming tea Helga put in front of her. Two banana-nut muffins joined the tea, a pretty gingham napkin was put beside her hand and a nosegay of cinnamon sticks tied with straw was laid in front of her china plate for decoration.

Though she was tired physically and mentally, Clove realized she felt at home and welcome.

"Eat," Helga said in her German accent. "For babies."

Clove nodded, and as Helga draped a crocheted shawl over her shoulders, she knew Archer had—again—not been bragging in his e-mails.

This really was a special family. A special place.

"You are first girl Archer brings home," Helga said.

Clove started. "Ever?"

"Yes. While I've lived here. The brothers say he is too much afraid to like a girl."

"Why?"

"Because." Helga looked at her. "His mother died when he was very young. All he knew was that she went away and never came back. They say he is always afraid of that."

"Oh." Clove blinked.

"So you won't leave."

It was a question couched in a statement. Clove's skin prickled as Helga's worried gaze searched hers.

After a moment, Helga turned back to stir something on the stove. And Clove looked out the big kitchen window, seeing the spring, still-unawakened landscape, and the two big men standing outside talking more with their hands than with their mouths.

They weren't so taciturn—and they weren't so unruly, either. Right now, Archer seemed to be on the receiving end of whatever Mason was saying.

Clove turned away, knowing that she was the topic of their conversation. Unexpected and not yet considered a blessing, she figured she was about as trusted as Tonk.

"THERE'S JUST NO WAY around it," Mason said sternly. "You have to marry her."

"Mason, trust me, it's just not going to happen," Archer replied. "She'd yell so loud if you said that to her they'd hear her in the next county."

"How do I have two brothers get women pregnant out of wedlock," Mason roared. "Both with women who do not want them? Is there a chance that I've done something wrong? Did I miss a concept? You should be in love to make babies! It works better that way!"

"Admittedly. But I'm working on her."

"Working on marrying her?"

"No. Working on getting her to fall in love with me."

Mason stared at him. "Can I ask you why you got her pregnant if you knew you weren't in love with each other?"

"I thought she was fine."

"Well, clearly," Mason said with disgust. "She is fine. But that's no reason to knock someone up. Consensual sex with a lady who is fine is no reason to just uncork the—"

"Mason. I thought she was 'fine' as in 'on birth control.' She said she was fine, and clearly we have two different meanings of that word."

"That's what happens when you meet people who are not from your background," Mason said. "You have to overcome a host of communication issues, and one of them is language differences. So you didn't ask her to elaborate on her 'fineness.' You just dived right in."

Archer frowned. "Mason, it's all irrelevant now."

"Except that she won't marry you. That makes it pathetic. We are not having three children out of wedlock!"

"One is better than three?"

"Well, don't you think it's a bit odd?" Mason demanded. "It's like, here's my mistake, times three!"

"I really don't feel like it's a mistake."

"Oh, it's not a mistake to be having children by someone you've just met."

"Not everybody takes their whole lifetime to acknowledge a good woman, Mason," Archer said stiffly.

Mason blinked. "I'm going to overlook that," he said, his voice low.

"Well, you overlook a lot. Now, for the moment, you and I need to agree that we're not on the same page about my marital status. Clove has been to the doctor today, and she's tired. I'd like to go make her feel at home."

Mason raised his eyebrows. "And where do you expect to take her?"

"To one of the houses. I don't care which."

"Has it ever occurred to you that Miss Penmire might prefer to be married? Have you asked her?"

"I've mentioned it, but I told you, she's not interested in staying here. I'm going to try to change her mind, but she's a decisive little thing."

"Three babies," Mason said. "I can't believe it."

"Neither can I. Or Clove."

Mason shook his head. "All right. I have a plan."

Archer's eyes widened. "What do you mean?"

"You're clearly out of options with this gal. You want her?"

"Of course," Archer said without hesitation. "In my heart, I know she is right for me. You learn a lot when you write someone for two years. Despite the fact that she came here on a mission, I'd like to give her more than just babies. I'd like to give her my name."

"Then what I propose is this. I'll discuss it with the boys later, but for now, my first thought is that we buy Mimi's house and land."

Archer looked at Mason, astonished. "We already have five thousand acres, and we only have six of twelve brothers working the ranch. Not to mention, I mean…" *Are you giving Mimi up that easily?* he wanted to shout.

"You're wanting a way to stay here, and Clove and you have three babies on the way. We'll need land for future generations."

Archer slowly took in what his older brother was saying. "Are you saying we buy Mimi's place for Clove?"

"For our babies," Mason said. "The way we're popping out all over here, this ranch isn't big enough for all of us. I have to think of the economics of future generations. How will we send them to college? What will we buy their wedding dresses with?

"I ran a forward proposal the other night on the costs this ranch is running, with wedding gowns, educations, braces, college—these are just the basics for each child in the family—and we're going to have to expand. Tighten up.

"Mimi's place is ideal for two reasons. One, we know it's a good property. The sheriff kept that place right. Also, we know ranch land here will appreciate. We'll have more space to branch out, and I haven't decided yet if that means cattle or agriculture, or something entirely different. For the moment, I think we buy it, keep strangers from moving in who may give us trouble over the pond, and offer the house to Clove. I don't see her and three babies fitting into any of our available scenarios. But Mimi's place is just right."

"Clove said they already have a farm of some type in Australia," Archer said.

"Yes, but this is Texas land, next to her Texas family, where the Texas man she wanted so bad lives."

"True, but her ties to her home are pretty strong," Archer said, thinking of the inscription on the back of the picture. "She and her sister are very close."

"As her husband, you'll be closer," Mason said.

"I don't know. She was pretty desperate to have children for Lucy."

Mason's eyebrows shot into his hair. "What are you talking about?"

"Clove claims she's giving the children to her sister to raise."

"Have you gone stark raving mad?" Mason demanded.

"I didn't say I like it—"

"I know you don't! Well, figure out a way to make her change her mind. Those children are staying here. There's no other way for it to be. Their Jefferson birthright is on this ranch."

Archer shook his head. "I completely agree. I just don't know how to get Clove to see it that way, and I'm not sure that a house is what would make her look favorably on me. Clove's extremely independent."

"And you're an extreme wuss. Get back to her and win her heart. Surely you are not going to be the only brother in this family who can't get his girl."

"No, I'm not." Archer glared. "I'm looking at the other brother who can't."

He strode away to find Clove.

She was morosely eating a muffin, looking as if she'd lost her best friend. She stood when he walked into the kitchen.

"Earlier you asked me a question," Clove said.

Archer blinked. "I'm kind of lost on the question. There's been so much drama. Could you refresh me?"

She took a deep breath. "You asked me, your bed or mine?"

Archer perked up at the mention of beds. "So I did. Yes, I did. Do you have an answer?"

She nodded. "I do. I'd like to stay in a hotel in Union Junction. I called my sister, Lucy, and she will be here tomorrow to stay with me until my visa runs out."

He looked down for a moment, thinking about Mason's words. Mason could not win his woman, and he was willing to give her house to Clove and the babies they were expecting. Frankly, he had not expected Mason to back him to this extent, given the reaction he'd had to Last's baby.

Of course, this situation was entirely different from anything the brothers had experienced so far.

"I'm glad your sister is coming to be with you," he said carefully, "but I'd feel bad for the two of you to be in a strange town with no one you know. There's plenty of room here for the two of you to have time alone."

She looked at him for a long moment. He saw something in her eyes change. "Are you sure?"

"Absolutely," he said, feeling hopeful that he might be targeting what was bothering her. "But right now, I'm going to tuck you into bed."

Chapter Ten

"We have three houses, and Calhoun built his own on the property," Archer said. "We juggle houses when necessary. Right now, Valentine, Last's ex-girlfriend, is living in one of them with their child. Valentine would be glad to let you stay there. Knowing you might feel awkward about that, and figuring you might like a very quiet place to completely relax, I would also like to propose the foreman's shack. Well, we call it a shack, but it's a modest bungalow. Very homey."

"Where will the foreman go?" Clove asked.

"Oh, we don't have one anymore. I mean, we're about to hire some extra help, since we're down so many brothers, but no one's living there now. Every once in a while, Shoeshine Johnson comes out to give us a hand, and he likes staying in the bungalow. He's a real good farmer, and bus driver, and he knows bulls. So we use him when he's available. But he's not here now. As I say, the place is simple, but I like it. There's a VCR and a video collection. Nothing on DVD yet, but…"

She smiled at him. "I'd feel very comfortable there. Thank you."

"I thought so. It's probably hard to be around strangers."

"Archer…you and your family are being very kind, considering…everything."

He nodded. "Let's get you resting."

She walked behind him as he took her bag. He reached back and put his arm around her shoulder, guiding her down the porch toward the truck.

"I'm all right," she said.

"I know, but something about becoming a father to three makes me feel protective." He grinned, opening the truck door for her. "I don't think my brothers thought I had it in me. For fatherhood, that is. How are you feeling, by the way?"

"A bit tired, actually."

"Well, you're about to feel a lot better. You're going to rest a lot, just like Dr. Edna Fern said." He shuddered and started the truck. "I still can't get over that name."

"Archer isn't the world's most common name."

"Nor is Clove, when you think about it. Or Clover." He frowned. "What would you have done if your plan hadn't worked?"

"Truthfully, I don't know. Now that the consequences have come home to me, I wish I hadn't done it at all." She looked down at her hands. "I changed your life and I didn't mean to. I think I would go to a sperm bank. That's what I would do."

He stared at her. "And miss out on all that fun?"

"It's not fun for you or your family."

"Actually, I meant the making love part. That was fun."

"But over so quickly. You know what I mean?" She looked at him, her eyes wide.

He couldn't believe his ears. "I was trying to be gentle since it was your first time."

"Oh." She blinked. "You mean it gets better?"

"Well, yes." He wasn't sure if his pride was hurt or not, and he decided he needed to overlook his ego screaming at the insult. "I'll give you the chance to try to wear me out in a few days. When you're feeling better."

She shook her head at him. "My sister will be here."

"Did you ever consider that I might have some restraint?" he asked.

"No," she said.

"Don't tell me you're one of those women who believe that men are solely interested in their own sexual pleasure?"

"Well, yes," Clove said. "You know, you did share an awful lot about yours and your brother's exploits."

"Yeah." He frowned at her. "I am mad at you, just for the record. Personally, I think it's wrong to make love to a man, get pregnant and not tell him. I know a lot of single guys would debate that with me. They'd love it if a woman kept that news to herself. Kind of spoils the routine, you see."

"Yes, I do," she said dryly.

"But not me. I always want to be right in the thick of things. Here we are." He shut off the engine. "Simple, but peaceful. Just what Dr. Edna would recommend."

She looked at the serene bungalow, then at him. "Thank you so much," she said, "for everything."

"You're welcome."

"I just don't understand why you're so nice about it all."

He sighed and pushed his hat back on his head. "Look. I'm kind of a floater. I'm too far down in the family food chain to understand huge pressure. I watched my twin, Ranger, fall in love with a saucy young lady, and he had a helluva good time doing it. You might say it was an adventure for all of us. Now, I guess I'm on my own adventure. You hit me between the eyes—"

"Legs," she reminded him. "But it was an accident."

"That's right! I'm still mad at you about that, too!" But he shrugged at her. "The fact is, if this is my adventure, then I want to enjoy mine as much as he did his. Well, some days it looked like Ranger was having fun, and other days he looked like he was pretty confused. My twin is happy now, though. You and I are bound together forever by three little bundles of joy, and I want us to get off on the right foot. If our feet don't end up at the altar, so be it. But let's have fun together." He thought about that for a minute. "I'm sure it's best for the children if we're laughing instead of bickering."

She nodded. "Okay."

"So, on to movie watching. Let's get you tucked up in bed, and then we're going to watch *Batman!*"

He saw her pucker.

"The one with Michael Keaton? Lots of stunt work," he said hopefully.

She got out of the truck and walked toward the bungalow. Grabbing her case, he hurried after her. "My second choice would be *The Adventures of Mr. Bean.* Not dangerous stunt work, but I do love economical humor. How about that?"

She smiled and followed him inside after he unlocked the door. "Oh, it's so homey," she said. "I love the fireplace! And the plaid blankets, and the deer wallpaper—is that a real armadillo?"

"Yes, it is," he said proudly. "And this is a real deer head, and this is a real squirrel and this is a real mountain lion. We're very proud of him."

She shivered. "It's not very pretty, is it?"

He looked at the mountain lion with some bemusement before taking in her round-eyed expression. "I guess not. You know, I think I'll move these critters into the attic. Make yourself comfy, and pick a movie you want to watch."

Quickly, he put his old friends away and hurried down the stairs. "What did you find?"

She held up a video. "Is this what they call a girlie film?"

"Girlie?" He read the label, feeling himself blush. "Er, it's a guy film. We don't need to watch that."

"But it's *Suzanne and the Gunslingers.* I think that sounds adventurous."

"No." He hid it behind the other fifty videos they had. "This may be a problem," he said. "We moved the VHS machine here when the DVDs came out because we figured we could watch the old stuff when we came here.

Sometimes we use this place as a hunting lodge, when Shoeshine's not on the ranch. In fact, I think that's *his* girlie movie!"

She laughed. "It is not. Poor Shoeshine."

"I'm certain he left it here," Archer said innocently. "Now, how about…*Silence of the Lambs*? Or even *Braveheart*? It has stunt work—"

"Here's one." Clove pulled it out and smiled at him. "And look. This one actually does have Shoeshine Johnson's name on it."

Archer took the video from her. "*Driving Miss Daisy*," he said. "Clove, I don't think there's much stunt work in this one."

She nodded. "I know. I'm kind of unplugging from the job right now."

He gulped. "I guess Shoeshine doesn't unplug from his. Wouldn't you know he'd leave behind the one movie about driving somebody. And it doesn't sound like anything explodes, gets naked and or has espionage in it."

"Which makes it perfect for relaxing."

He was pretty certain he'd gnaw his nails off from boredom. But if this movie was what Miss Clove wanted, then that's what she'd get.

A knock sounded on the door. They glanced at each other.

"Are you expecting company?" Archer asked.

"No. Not until tomorrow."

He opened the door. Mason stood there, carrying two sacks. Bandera was carting drinks from the truck, and Crockett carried firewood.

"We figured you needed groceries," Mason said.

"Comfort food," Last said. "Beer, wine, juice, water. Beer and wine for the father-to-be. Water for the little mama." He grinned. "And firewood, in case this place has a chill on it since we don't keep the thermostat turned on when no one is here. Yes, it is a wee bit chilly."

Clove sank onto the sofa.

Archer felt a little overwhelmed by all his brothers' attention. "We're not exactly in the wilderness."

"Still," Bandera said cheerfully, stacking drinks in the fridge, "when there's no sustenance, you might start imagining you're looking for locusts and honey. And we even brought Ben & Jerry's ice cream," he said with a satisfied smile, "and pickles. We figured we'd save you the midnight run to the grocery, Archer."

Archer glanced at Clove. She was torn, it seemed, between amusement and mortification. "They're my family," he said apologetically. "We've always been a bit overwhelming."

"How are you feeling, Miss Clove?" Crockett asked.

"I'm just ready to sit down and watch *Driving Miss Daisy*. That's what Archer chose for us to watch."

"Archer?" Bandera looked at him with surprise. "Our resident nonromantic?"

"Where's Last?" Archer demanded. "Just wondering, since the rest of you rode to our rescue."

"He's talking to Mimi, on behalf of Mason, the emotional chicken," Crockett said.

"Hey!" Mason yelled.

Crockett shrugged. "Last will be right here. Helga

made brownies, so we put a plate on the counter for you." He frowned, looking around the room. "Where are all the friendly beasts?"

"Residing in the attic for the moment." Archer gave him the raised eyebrow signifying *discuss later.*

"Can we talk to you for a moment, Clove?" Mason asked. "On a more serious matter. We won't take up much of your time."

"All right."

"Give her time to change," Archer growled. "She's supposed to be resting. Can't this wait until tomorrow?"

"I think we should talk tonight." Mason looked at the brothers, and they all nodded.

"All right. Clove, take your time getting ready. We'll all sit here and drink a beer."

"Thank you." She disappeared into a bedroom, then came back out. "Which bedroom is mine, Archer?"

All the brothers glared at him. Archer blinked. *Wherever mine is,* he thought, but didn't say it. "You choose," he said. "I'm easy."

He wasn't, but for the moment, he would ignore the pounding in his chest. He needed to get his brothers out of here so that he could have time alone with Clove, before Lucy arrived and he lost the chance to bond with the mother of his children.

MASON CLEARED his throat after Clove left the room. "Archer, we'd like to talk to you as a family."

"Go right ahead," Archer said. "I'm listening."

"We want you to work hard at making an honest woman of Clove."

"What the hell do you think I'm trying to do?" Archer demanded. "I'm watching chick flicks. I've hidden our best hunting trophies. I'm working on the situation. I'm sure I have it well in hand."

"We think you could wind up in a dodgy situation, when her sister arrives. Clove told Helga she was returning to Australia with Lucy," Mason said. "That's not the best thing for our babies."

"*Our* babies?" Archer stared at his brother. "Since when did you become the welcome committee for tiny beings wearing diapers?"

"Since you're having three of them, and they're yours," Mason said. "Ours."

"And what was Last's baby?" Archer demanded.

"Well, there were too many questions up front," Mason said. "He wasn't sure about this, and he wasn't certain about that. Made it hard to get excited about the baby when he wasn't paying attention to whether it was his or not. We've rectified that since then, and Last's bundle of joy gets plenty of uncle love. But in your case, you know you're having children with Clove, especially as she set out to lure you to the bassinet." He wrinkled his forehead. "I suppose that would be plural now. Bassinets."

"Okay, okay." Archer rubbed his face. "So what? You're all here to team up with me to convince her that life here is just what she's always dreamed of? Come on, Mason. Life here isn't what anybody dreams of, apparently. Everybody up and left as soon as they found a bride. Except Calhoun, but there were extenuating circumstances there."

"We're more than shorthanded now, Archer," Mason concurred. "We can't have you jetting off to Australia to lie on the golden beaches and chase little joeys. We need you here. You're going to have to make certain you don't mess this up. Last has gone to make an offer on Mimi's house and land. Before it goes on the market to the general public."

"*Last* did? Is there something wrong with *your* mouth?" Archer glanced at his brothers incredulously. Crockett and Bandera shifted uncomfortably, staring out windows as they leaned against walls. "Are you the world's biggest yellowbelly? How can you sit here and lecture me when the best thing that's ever going to happen to you is moving off her family ranch into town where you'll actually have to make an effort to see her, the baby and the sheriff?"

"Archer," Mason said on a growl, "you're mouthing off about stuff you know nothing about."

"Peace, brothers," Crockett interrupted. "Let's get on with the business at hand. Archer, Last is making an offer to Mimi that's fair. As the member of the family who can get the job done with a minimum of wrangling, not to mention hard feelings, we felt Last was the proper one to offer. We want you to make an offer to Clove. Mimi's house for her and her children so that she'll feel comfortable staying here." He took a deep breath. "It's the right thing to do, Archer. You got her into this boat—or vice versa—but she has no choice but to return to Australia, unwed and her children fatherless, unless you act."

"You know," Archer said, "I would like to act. I really, really would. But it's hard when you show up acting like all Clove needs is a roof over her head. I'm telling you, this girl is not that simple. This is not a scheme on her behalf to hook me. She does not want me. She is not acting out of a desire to be with me for the rest of life as we know it. I wish it were that easy. I could have all the gold in the world and she would not be one whit more interested in me than she is at this moment." He frowned. "Hang on. Clove's gotten very quiet."

He strode off to find her. The bedroom door open, she obviously felt no need to act as if she wasn't listening to their conversation. And indeed, she wasn't, he realized, as she was fast asleep in a bed with a set of deer antlers as a canopy. He sighed and closed her door.

Rejoining his brothers, he said, "Everybody out. Thank you for your concern and worry, but my girl has had a very rough day. She can't handle intrigues and house offers. The doctor says she needs rest and that is what she is going to have. You're jumping the gun, anyway. If she doesn't get rest, who knows if she'll carry these children to term. I don't understand enough about pregnancy to know, but my guess is it's a good idea to follow doc's orders. Thank you for the food—I'll take very good care of her. Good night."

After a moment of glancing at each other, his brothers silently filed out, their faces downcast. They meant well, Archer knew, but Clove required the kind of handling they would never understand.

When the house was empty, he turned off the porch lights. Miss Daisy would have to wait for another day, so he put the tape away and returned the sofa pillows to their proper positions. As all the groceries were stored, he headed to Clove's chosen room. Pulling off his boots and stripping to his boxers, he crawled in bed beside her, sighing as his chilly skin was warmed by hers. In her sleep, she rolled over, putting one hand on his chest and her cheek on his shoulder. Closing his eyes, Archer's chest relaxed, all the pressure he'd been feeling melting away.

This was heaven.

But then she stirred against him, tucking herself up under his chin. His eyes widened in the darkness.

"Archer?" she murmured.

"Yes. What is it?" he asked, suddenly worried that she wasn't feeling well.

"Do you ever wonder if…what might happen if it's not just our blood types that are incompatible?"

He blinked. "No."

"Oh."

None of this sounded good. "Do you wonder?" he asked.

"Sort of," she whispered. "I mean, we had sex and that's pretty cut-and-dried. But people have to be really compatible if there's going to be anything else."

So there was a chance. She was thinking about the future, wondering what it held in store for them. He thought about Last and Valentine. No compatibility for the long haul there, so Clove had a good point. "Go to sleep," he said. "We don't have to have all the answers tonight. You're supposed to be resting happily and thinking good thoughts. Not worrying."

"I'm not worrying," she said softly. "I just don't see us being compatible."

Well, she'd been right about everything until now. Gently, he rolled her onto her back. He stroked her face with his palm. "Can you see me?"

"No."

"I can't see you, either. That means this is a blind compatibility test." Then he kissed her. Softly at first, then more deeply when she didn't resist. When her lips touched his more urgently and he felt her tongue experimentally touch his, he kissed her harder, faster, his mouth moving against hers in a sexual mating dance that had her moaning beneath him.

She cried out, a small, surprised squeal against his lips, her fingers suddenly clutching at his shoulders. He pulled back in alarm. "Are you all right?"

"Yes," she said, her voice astonished in the darkness.

"Are you sure?"

She took a moment to answer, her hands sliding down his arms. "I think so. Give me a couple seconds to figure it out."

He frowned. "Figure what out?"

"I think I just…you know."

He passed a hand across her stomach. "Tell me."

"Had a climax," she whispered, then giggled.

Relief swept over him. He rolled over onto his side, saying gruffly, "Go to sleep. The babies probably wish you'd settle down. The doctor said we weren't supposed to have relations, and I assume that means all forms of pleasure."

He felt her turn over. A sigh left his chest, the worry lifting from him. That crazy little giggle floated across his memory, and he grinned to himself in the darkness. "Guess you answered the compatibility question, though."

She gave a little backward kick, her heel lightly grazing his calf, which made him chuckle. "We can run a retest tomorrow, if you'd like."

"Archer!"

He laughed.

ARCHER WAS SLEEPING like a dog until his senses warned him something was different from the easy comfort he'd been enjoying last night. Keeping his eyes closed, he assessed his surroundings. Warm, soft body next to him—check. In fact, Clove's hand lay dangerously close to his maleness, and if not for the sheet, he'd be getting pretty close to happiness. His body acknowledged this fact, slowly stirring up an erection.

But his mind countered his desire. Something was still not right.

His eyes snapped open, to find a stunningly lovely woman staring at him from the foot of the bed. "Hello," she said.

"Crap!" He jumped from the bed, startling Clove. She sat straight up, clutching the sheet.

The Harlequin Reader Service® — Here's how it works:

Accepting your 2 free books and gift places you under no obligation to buy anything. You may keep the books and gift and return the shipping statement marked "cancel." If you do not cancel, about a month later we'll send you 4 additional books and bill you just $4.24 each in the U.S., or $4.99 each in Canada, plus 25¢ shipping & handling per book and applicable taxes if any.* That's the complete price and — compared to cover prices of $4.99 each in the U.S. and $5.99 each in Canada — it's quite a bargain! You may cancel at any time, but if you choose to continue, every month we'll send you 4 more books, which you may either purchase at the discount price or return to us and cancel your subscription.
*Terms and prices subject to change without notice. Sales tax applicable in N.Y. Canadian residents will be charged applicable provincial taxes and GST. Credit or debit balances in a customer's account(s) may be offset by any other outstanding balance owed by or to the customer.

If offer card is missing write to: Harlequin Reader Service, 3010 Walden Ave., P.O. Box 1867, Buffalo NY 14240-1867

NO POSTAGE
NECESSARY
IF MAILED
IN THE
UNITED STATES

BUSINESS REPLY MAIL
FIRST-CLASS MAIL   PERMIT NO. 717-003   BUFFALO, NY

POSTAGE WILL BE PAID BY ADDRESSEE

HARLEQUIN READER SERVICE
3010 WALDEN AVE
PO BOX 1867
BUFFALO NY 14240-9952

GET FREE BOOKS and a FREE GIFT WHEN YOU PLAY THE...

Lucky 7

SLOT MACHINE GAME!

Just scratch off the silver box with a coin. Then check below to see the gifts you get!

YES! I have scratched off the silver box. Please send me the 2 free Harlequin American Romance® books and gift for which I qualify. I understand I am under no obligation to purchase any books, as explained on the back of this card.

354 HDL D36C   **154 HDL D36S**

FIRST NAME

LAST NAME

ADDRESS

APT.#

CITY

STATE/PROV.

ZIP/POSTAL CODE

7 7 7	Worth TWO FREE BOOKS plus a BONUS Mystery Gift!
🍒 🍒 🍒	Worth TWO FREE BOOKS!
♣ ♣ ♣	Worth ONE FREE BOOK!
🔔 🔔 🔔	TRY AGAIN!

www.eHarlequin.com

(H-AR-02/05)

DETACH AND MAIL CARD TODAY!

"Lucy!" Clove jumped from the bed, rushing to hug her sister. "Why didn't you call me? I would have met you at the airport!"

Lucy eyed him over Clove's shoulder as they embraced. Archer stared right back at her, until he realized he was wearing nothing but black boxers and this was no way to meet his children's auntie for the first time. Grabbing his jeans, he jerked them on, never taking his eyes off Lucy. For added composure, he snatched his cowboy hat off the headboard and jammed that on his head.

"My taxi driver knew exactly where the ranch was," Lucy said, in a voice much like Clove's. "And then the man I met at the ranch said I'd find you here. So the taxi driver brought me. The door was unlocked," she said, more to Archer than anyone. "I assumed you were awake and about, but when I called out, no one answered. So I came on in. Of course, I expected you to be alone, Clove," she said, her tone slightly surprised but not necessarily disapproving, Archer noticed.

"I'll get us a cup of joe," he said, retreating. "Clove, can you drink coffee? Or do you have to have water or juice or something healthy?"

"Orange juice, please," Clove replied. "Lucy, this is Archer Jefferson."

The sisters moved out of their embrace so that Lucy could shake Archer's hand. He wasn't certain how he felt about that, since he didn't have a shirt or boots on, and this was Clove's sister. And she was gorgeous like a movie star, though he suspected it was all natural. "Sorry I'm not clean-shaven," he said, trying to be polite.

"It's fine," Lucy replied. "I had visions of Clove being alone. I'm happy to see she's been in good hands."

Uncomfortable, he merely nodded, retreating to the kitchen so the ladies could talk. He fixed coffee, his mind racing. So this was the Lucy who couldn't have children, the sister Clove loved more than anything. She certainly hadn't seemed to be hurting for money, style or manners. Scratching at his chest, he thought about Clove's determination to help her sister. He would help his brothers if they needed him to, but there was something deeper between the two women. Perhaps because there had been so many brothers in his family, they had shared the bonding and emotions equally amongst all of them, so that it seemed less intense. Would he have a child for one of them? He didn't think so.

Of course, it was a little hard to compare, because he didn't hold the key of creation within his body. Other than the sperm donation, the male of the species got off pretty light. He wondered how much heart a woman had to have to use her body to help her sister.

Lucy walked into the kitchen, picking up a coffee mug and pouring herself a cup. She looked at him, her gaze frank.

"Cream? Sugar?" he asked.

"No, thank you." She sipped the coffee, her eyes gauging him over the rim.

"Long flight?" he asked.

"Very long, but not bad. The prospect of visiting my sister kept me from noticing any discomforts."

He nodded. "Where is Clove?"

"Showering. She said she hadn't had a chance to last night."

"It was a long day for her."

Lucy put her mug down. "So what does the doctor say, exactly?"

"That she needs rest. And possibly another round of whatever that injection was to keep our Rh factors compatible. Mostly rest."

Lucy went a bit pale. "Is it likely or unlikely that she'd miscarry?"

"With rest and care, her chances going full term are pretty good." Archer shrugged. "The next couple of days are pretty important for her." He looked at her, his gaze curious. "So. I guess you really wanted to be a mother for Clove to have gotten pregnant."

"This was not my idea," Lucy snapped. "I didn't know Clove was trying to help me like this. When I put her on the plane in Australia, she told me she was coming to America to see the world. She needed to unwind from stunt work. That was it."

"Sorry." Archer took a deep breath. "I know Clove well enough to know that she would take the path she thought best and not consult a soul."

"Clove has always been brave. Very kind and generous." Lucy looked at him. "Not to put too fine a point on it, but the last thing I expected to find was a cowboy in my sister's bed."

The lady was inquiring, he figured, and a man should always be honest. "Fine points don't trouble me," he said mildly. "And, with all due respect, I hope you realize that I'll be doing everything in my power to *stay* in Clove's bed."

Chapter Eleven

"And if she doesn't want you in her bed?" Lucy asked Archer.

He smiled. "We're very, very compatible."

"You're not at all what I expected," Lucy said.

"I could say the same," Archer replied, pouring himself another cup of coffee.

"So you didn't just balk when you found out my sister was pregnant? Have your way with her and then go on?"

He dug around for some bagels his brothers had put away. "No, ma'am. Do I look like that sort to you?"

She sighed and took the plate of bagel and red grapes he offered her. "Thank you. Then I don't understand. If your intentions are to care for my sister, why is she returning to Australia?"

"You'd know the answer to that better than me."

"I meant, without you," Lucy said. "Why is she returning without you?"

"This is my home," Archer said simply. "I'm not planning to leave it. And she hasn't invited me. She wasn't planning to tell me she was pregnant."

Lucy put her plate down, her fingers trembling. "I guess Clove told you that I—"

"She did," Archer said swiftly, his tone kind. "I don't need further details."

She glanced down for a moment. "Did she also tell you that my husband and I—"

"She mentioned something about it."

"I see." Lucy bit her lip, clearly humiliated. "I guess she told you that the farm isn't doing well."

He shook his head.

"It's ours," she said. "Mine and Clove's. My husband is a doctor and doesn't know a lot about such things. We don't ask him for money for the farm. It's ours, and it's all we have left between us. We're adopted," Lucy said quietly. "Did she tell you that, too?"

"No." Archer's mind scrambled to keep up with that information. "Clove and I really haven't had a chance to get to know each other to that extent."

She blushed. "This is very awkward."

"You're telling me." But he was starting to understand Clove's desperation better.

"Good morning," Clove said, walking to stand beside her sister. They hugged each other briefly around the waist, then Clove sighed over the bagel and grapes her sister held. "Would you mind if I have some of that?" she asked Archer.

He grabbed a plate. "Feeding you well was what my brothers had in mind." With two plump stems of red grapes beside a bagel, he handed her the plate.

"Glad to see you with an appetite." After he'd poured

a glass of apple juice, he said, "I'm going to head out. You two will enjoy being alone for a while. Lucy, I have work to do. I'm sure you can take over here."

Lucy nodded, her eyes grateful. "I can."

"All right." He went into the bedroom, grabbed his shirt, put on his boots and slipped on his belt before walking back out of the bedroom. "I've got an Appaloosa that wants breakfast, too," he told the women, "and she gets ornery if her food isn't right on time."

Clove looked at him, her gaze a bit nervous. "Say hello to Tonk for me."

He was pleased that she still thought kindly of his horse. "I will. Nice to meet you, Lucy." Tipping his hat, he left, thinking it was a great time to get out and clear his head.

Between his brothers trying to buy Mimi's house for Clove, and Lucy's small, elegant satchel that foretold her plans for a very short visit to Texas, he had a lot to think about.

He did not want to lose Clove, not when she'd started getting under his skin in the kind of way no other woman ever had.

LUCY TURNED TO CLOVE after Archer left. "So. You left out some important details," she said. "Let's sit on this nice, terribly western sofa and you can fill in the story."

"Starting with?" Clove followed Lucy to the sofa, plate and cup in hand.

"The fact that you just happened to land one of the most handsome men on the planet."

Clove shook her head. "Archer would smirk at both your description of him and the notion that he's been landed."

"I don't know. He seems…interested in you."

"Archer's hard to explain. I wouldn't be overly impressed with his interest."

"And you met him how?"

Clove looked at her sister. "Over the Internet. We've corresponded for two years."

Lucy thought about that for a moment. "So, in light of the fact that you came straight to Texas and haven't ventured from your original destination, I can assume that your trip was less about seeing the world than about seeing this cowboy. Those must have been some e-mails."

Clove shrugged. "They were pretty tame, actually."

"Did he know you were coming to meet him?"

She shook her head. "No. I didn't tell him my real name. I wanted to meet him first."

"Good move. That first meeting must have been impressive."

Clove looked at her sister carefully. "He was more attractive than I thought he'd be, certainly."

"I'll say." Lucy laughed. "And so you met him, gave him a fake name for safety's sake, and he seduced you?"

"I seduced him."

Lucy laughed at her. "Clove. Not you."

"Yes. Me."

The smile slipped from Lucy's face. She stared at her sister for a long moment. "All right. Let me run through this again. You flew around the world to meet this man, and decided to seduce him, and then called me and told me you wanted me to raise your children." She frowned. "It's not like you to act so crazily."

Clove was silent for a moment. "Stunt work."

"No." Lucy shook her head. "Those are calculated risks. You threw yourself out on a huge limb for no reason that I can see. This makes no sense." She stared at Clove for a long moment. "No, wait a moment. You decided to get pregnant and give me the children to save my marriage because I couldn't have any? Is that closer to the real crazy truth? That's the idea that cowboy seems to be peddling."

Clove sighed. "Lucy, as wild as it sounds, it's not unusual for women to use a surrogate mother. That's all I wanted to be."

Tears welled in Lucy's eyes, which she wiped away. "First of all, honey, you can't take advantage of this poor man because of me. You're going to have to tell him the truth. I think he's falling in love with you. Or something. He certainly seems fond of you, and quite concerned for your well-being."

"He knows the truth."

"He does? And he's not angry with you?"

"I would say that his anger is overridden by his determination to make certain his children stay here. Also, his brothers agree with Archer's tactics. They came here to talk to me last night but I fell asleep." She sighed. "It had been a long, scary day. Archer and I have incompatible Rh factors, and I'd had some cramping. Now he's even more determined to protect me and his children."

"I see. Well," Lucy said, "considering that he's had fatherhood sprung on him, he's being damn responsible."

Clove nodded. "Yes."

Lucy took a long drink of coffee. "Secondly, you can't interfere in my life without asking me. I don't want to be a mother this way."

Clove was shocked. "Lucy!"

Lucy shook her head. "It's true. I'm sorry, and it's going to sound mean, but I wanted my own children. Mine and Robert's. But if it's not meant to be, it's not meant to be. I can accept that. I also accept that my husband is going to leave me."

"Don't say that!"

"I can say it because he already has." Lucy's eyes welled up again. "And I can be more honest and say that our problems go deeper than my inability to conceive. Robert says he feels overwhelmed by marriage to me. I don't think bringing triplets into the picture is going to help him."

"I don't understand. Robert loves you. I honestly thought he just wanted to be a father so badly that he—"

"Robert does love me. But the fertility problem lies with him." Lucy swallowed, her eyes full of pain. "I always say that I cannot conceive for his benefit. The truth is, the doctors say—and these are associates of his—there's a problem with his sperm."

Clove put her arms around her sister. "I'm so sorry. Aren't there procedures for that?"

"There are. And we recently tried one. It didn't take. I believe that was a breaking point for Robert." She hugged Clove, burying her face in her hair. "Thank you for trying to make my dreams come true, Clove. But you can't save my marriage, honey. You can't make a man feel things he doesn't, and you can't change what a man feels about himself."

Clove felt tears well in her eyes but she was determined not to let her sister see them. Lucy had already been through enough. "I wish I'd been there for you."

"Actually, it was time for Robert and I to face this by ourselves. While he loves you, he feels that I pay more attention to you sometimes than I do him." Lucy laughed a little. "Since he works odd hours, it's probably true."

"I didn't know he felt that way."

"Oh, well." Lucy pulled away, leaning her head back against the sofa to look at the ceiling. "I believe at the end he was just angry and saying things. Anything. People lash out when they're hurt. He feels that he's let me down." She rolled her head to look at her sister. "I'm glad I came to visit you. I wanted to tell you in person that Robert had left me, but I also needed to get away. It's so simple and comfortable here."

"It is." Clove sat next to her sister and put her head back on the sofa as well. "There's something very comfortable about Archer. He makes me feel better about everything."

"It's that lordly I've-got-everything-under-control attitude of his."

"Maybe. Although he really doesn't have everything under control, you know? His horse, for example. Tonk is tricky. And he likes that. I know from his e-mails that he likes rodeo, and there's no control in that. His family life—same thing. They're always out of control."

"It's an inner confidence he has. Very attractive. He has control of himself."

"That's true," Clove said with surprise. "I've never met a man so sure of himself. He just goes for it, with all his heart, when he wants something."

"Something you two have in common," Lucy said. "Heart. Inner confidence."

"I have no inner confidence."

"Right. You just leave home and go around the world to get pregnant so your sister's marriage will be saved. Clove, you're scarily brave. Just like Mom always said."

"Maybe she meant that I was an insane risk taker. I think she was just being polite."

"What are you going to do about him?" Lucy asked. "Now that you've taken this insane risk of trying to catch this cowboy?"

Clove rolled her head to look at her sister. "I am not trying to catch Archer. He wasn't remotely interested when he met me. We were together one night and accidentally hit the big bonanza, and I'm not sure which one of us was more stunned. Now he's determined to keep me here, but it's all about the babies."

"It's a start. Robert and I started our relationship with a rose," Lucy said thoughtfully. "A rose that led to a long courtship without sex. He saw me in a mall one day, gave me a rose and told me I was beautiful. I was still recovering from losing our adopted parents, and I'm afraid I jumped at the attention. Still, we didn't have relations right up until the night before we married. For you and Archer, sex came first. Maybe the love and the marriage will come later.

"Two years of correspondence is a pretty powerful getting-to-know-someone device. People generally write more than they say, especially men. They're tough on verbalizing their feelings sometimes." She blinked.

"One time, a long time ago," she confirmed softly, "Robert wrote me a love poem. It was the most beautiful thing I ever read. When he puts his feelings on paper, it's thrilling." She sat up, snatching the red grapes off her plate. "That was the only time he ever wrote me anything, though."

"I know we've discussed this before, but you're certain adoption isn't an option?" Clove asked, still disbelieving that her sister's marriage could be over.

"At this point, definitely not," Lucy said, "since there's no father in the picture. However, you and I were adopted, Clove. I...something in me wanted my very own flesh and blood. And Robert wasn't keen. I think... he didn't want to announce to the world that he couldn't—that we couldn't—get pregnant."

"I see." Clove took her sister's hand in hers, squeezing it. "I love you, Lucy. Thank you for coming here. I needed you."

"I needed you, too. I can't believe you're going to be a little mother!" Putting one hand on Clove's tummy, she laughed. "You're going to be the most beautiful mother in the world."

"Not me," Clove said. "That would have been you. Remember, I'm the dowdy little sister."

"If you believe that, you haven't looked in the mirror lately. Pregnancy—or something else—agrees with you." Lucy gave her a saucy wink. "Maybe it's Texas air that agrees with you. Or love."

Clove stood. "I'm going to take a nap. I don't know why I'm tired, because I slept hard last night."

"I don't know how you could sleep with that gorgeous man in your bed! I must admit I was completely surprised, Clove. My little sister in bed with a man!"

Clove blushed. "Archer tends to make himself at home."

Lucy laughed. "It's wonderful to be the object of a man's attentions."

Clove wasn't sure about that yet. "Wake me up in an hour, okay? I'm sorry to bug out on you, but I seem to get very—"

Lucy waved her hand. "Go on. I am going to sit here like a lady of leisure and enjoy my vacation by reading a magazine. And maybe cooking a little. The farm keeps me so busy that I never have time to relax."

Clove nodded, feeling guilty. "I shouldn't have left you with all the work."

"Well, it was time for you to get away, Clove. Truthfully, I'm happier about you than I've ever been. You always worked so hard. Always were older than your years. It's great to see you blossoming." Lucy smiled. "We'll figure something out about the farm later. Let's think about the babies first. Triplets, my word!"

Clove swung around. "Lucy! Robert left you when you told him I was having triplets, didn't he?"

Lucy looked at her.

"It's true, isn't it? That was the final straw?"

"Clove, infertility is infertility. He was happy you were pregnant—"

"But three babies. Not just one, but three. That made him feel bad, didn't it?"

She hesitated a second too long for Clove not to know she'd hit the truth. "Well, he may have been a bit hurt. I mean, it's probably hard on a man's self-esteem to know that his sister-in-law can have children but he can't give them to his—"

"So instead of helping your marriage, I ended it," Clove said frankly.

"Now, Clove," Lucy said, "we were already having troubles—"

"But that's when he finally left. I called you and told you about the babies and you were excited for me, and you told him, and he left."

"It doesn't matter, Clove. I really think he would have left eventually. The strains were tearing us apart."

"It matters to me, Lucy," Clove said, her heart breaking. "It matters more than anything to me."

Chapter Twelve

Two hours later, Archer let himself into the little bungalow. "Clove?" he called.

She came out from the bedroom wearing a pretty dress and a frown. "Yes?"

"Oh." He glanced around. "Where's Lucy?"

"Right here." Lucy walked to join her sister. "Hey, Archer."

"Is everything all right?" he asked, wondering why they looked so serious.

"Did you need something?" Clove asked, glancing around. "Did you leave your hat here?"

"No. I've got my hat." He was perplexed by her sad expression. Clearly, the sisters had an issue on their minds. "And I don't need anything. Are you okay?"

"Yes." She sighed. "We've been chatting. That's all."

Well, woman talk probably made women frown sometimes. "Well," he said, "can this little monster chat with y'all?" He pulled his hat from behind his back, and the little kitten Clove had adopted in Lonely Hearts Station popped her head up from inside, meowing.

"Tink!" Clove gasped, running to take the kitten from his hat. "Look, Lucy. This is my little kitty!" She rubbed Tink against her chin. "You're still so soft, Tink!"

Lucy gave Archer a droll look. "Nice, cowboy. Very nice."

He grinned. "Thank you."

"Thank you," Clove said. "I thought you didn't like cats!"

The grin slipped from his face, turning his expression uncomfortable. "I'm going to make a huge effort to like Tink. And she's going to make a huge effort not to be so fond of my hat. Aren't you, Tink?"

Tink cared about nothing except batting at Clove's earrings. She laughed. "I love this little ball of fur."

Lucy was still looking at Archer, he finally realized. "What?" he said to her.

"Just watching you do your thing, cowboy," she said.

"And it's a very good thing, too," he replied. "You two keep bonding. I'm off to haul in some feed."

"Bye, Archer," Clove said.

"How are you feeling, by the way?" he asked as he turned in the doorway. "Do you feel like eating at the big house tonight? I can drive you up and we can make it a quick evening. The boys would understand you couldn't make an all-nighter of it."

"I'd like that," Clove said. "Lucy?"

"It should be interesting," Lucy said, her eyebrow lifting.

Archer laughed. "Wait till you meet my brothers. They're even more interesting than me."

Clove smiled, waving Tink's paw at him. "Can you bring me an extra hat to transport Tink tonight? I think she feels at home in your hat, but I assume you don't always want to share such a conveyance with her."

"Sure." Archer settled a long look on her, taking in her dress and her hair, and last, her lips. "I'll be back around six," he said. "Call if you need anything."

He closed the door behind him.

"Whew," Lucy said. "He warmed the room twenty degrees with the way he looked at you!"

Clove blushed, thinking about the kiss they'd shared last night. He'd warmed her without trying to, in ways she didn't even know a woman could be warmed. "He's just sexy," Clove said. "It's not that he's doing anything extra for me."

Lucy was still staring at the door. "Clove, you've got to get down off your fence."

"What do you mean?"

"Either you want that sexy beast or you don't."

Clove sank onto the sofa and looked at her sister. "Lucy, it's not that simple. I didn't come to America to find a man. I could have found a man in Australia."

"But that hunk is here," Lucy said, "and it's time for you to figure out you've got one devilishly manly fellow trying his best to pay attention to you." She looked at the kitten sitting in Clove's lap, swatting at the buttons on her dress. "Men do not fetch kittens for women they're not interested in."

"It was nice of him."

"It was extraordinary. Makes me wonder what else

he has up his sleeve." Lucy smiled. "Kind of fun finding out, isn't it?"

"What do you mean?"

"I got the distinct impression that he intends to woo you until you go over to his side."

Clove's female pride flowered a little. "Did he say that?"

"In so many words, and then a few more. He seemed to think that anything standing in his way was only a flimsy challenge to his right and might. I like that in a man. I really do."

Clove sighed. "Lucy, if you had seen him when he first met me, there was no spark. No ember to burst into flame. It just wasn't there. And I wear baggy nightwear and dresses to hide the fact that I am beginning to lose my waist, and now he finds me attractive? I just don't buy it."

"Well, there are two things at work here that you probably don't understand. Men love babies. They may not tell you this, but they love the look of a woman carrying a baby, specifically when it's his baby. It's a proclamation to the whole world of his manhood. You're carrying three of his, and you can get as big as his barn, and he's just going to find you more attractive. This is how the men who are really worth loving act. There are the losers out there who don't get it. But real men love to see their woman blossoming."

"Eh," Clove said with distaste. "And the second thing at work?"

"Oh. Well, you may not want to let the mirror tell you

this, but you are more attractive now. You're filled out,
you look happy, rested…content. It just shows. And it
makes you more alluring to him. So don't think about
what happened when you first met him. Goodness,
Clove, not every love is destined to happen in the first
instant two people meet. Sometimes it's the ones that take
a long time that are the most tested and meaningful."

Lucy looked sad and Clove changed the subject. "So,
do we go eat with the boys?"

"Sure!" Lucy's eyes widened. "I'm nearly divorced.
I deserve an evening with attractive cowboys!"

"Lucy!"

Her sister laughed. "Oh, my goodness, quit being
such a silly. A girl can look and not touch, can't she?
What's the harm in that? Besides, I'm not a cowboy sort
of girl. I married a doctor who hated our farm. Doesn't
that tell you everything?"

Clove shook her head. "I don't know anymore."

"Don't be upset, Clove. There's so much good in
your life that I want you to enjoy it. Be happy."

"I'm trying," Clove said. "But right now, I'm just
looking forward to eating dessert tonight."

Lucy laughed. "That's my girl."

ARCHER WAS NERVOUS as he went to pick up Clove and
Lucy. He figured it had to do with the fact that tonight
felt oddly like a date; Lucy was somewhat parental
about Clove, and he and Clove had never truly had a
date. The picking-up and eating-with-the-family phase
was one they hadn't done before, so this had special

meaning. He straightened his bolo, hoping his brothers would behave in this first sit-down meal with his lady.

Just thinking about it made him more nervous. He worried about moving Clove from the bungalow for an hour, but surely eating a delicious meal Helga had prepared constituted resting. Then he wondered if he should take flowers for Clove. He fumbled with his hat and picked up a bucket for Tink that he'd spread a towel in for easy, clean, comfortable transport.

No, flowers would be seen as a sign of wooing on his part, and that would spook Clove. Delivering Tink had been enough. Dinner with his family would be a hurdle they should successfully cross before more was done.

Looking at his teeth, he slicked his hair once more.

"Nervous?" Last said, coming into his room.

Archer grunted.

Last leaned up against the wall. "You like this girl."

"What gives you that impression?" He checked his teeth. White, with maybe a small uneven crook on the side. He was shaven, except that his face always seemed a bit dark with stubble around his chin.

"You and I are the new dads in the family. Unexpected fatherhood is a bit of a jolt, isn't it?"

"I've had bigger jolts." Archer checked his fingernails to make certain no dirt resided beneath. "Should I wear cologne, or is that overdoing it?"

"Overdoing what?"

Archer met his brother's gaze. *"It."*

Last laughed. "Ah, you must mean the eager-swain routine."

"No, I don't mean that," Archer retorted. "I just don't want to be a dope."

Last shook his head. "You're a dope no matter what, as far as Mason's concerned. You didn't use a condom. Get over it. You cost the ranch money. Blah, blah, blah. You know the routine."

"I don't care," Archer said. "I like her. For the first time in my life, I really like someone."

Last nodded. "I know."

Archer stared at himself in the mirror. "It's as good as it's gonna get."

"I think she likes you fine, bro. By the way, Mimi accepted Mason's offer."

"Offer to what?" Archer frowned, still fiddling with his bolo.

"To buy her house and property."

Archer stopped fiddling and stared at his brother. "Just like that?"

"I guess so. I made the offer, and she said yes."

Archer thought about that. "Mason's letting her leave. Just like that."

"Archer, nothing is just like that. Especially not with Mason."

"Why did you make the offer and not him? I don't understand that."

"Because it's Mimi. Because he can't face her with any big decisions. You know him."

Archer chewed on that. "Something's fishy here. Mason didn't even blink when he learned Mimi was going to sell her place."

"He did. He threw his napkin down and left. But he knew it wouldn't do any good to steam over it. You know Mimi. When her mind's made up, it's all hell's-bustin'-loose. Mason figured we needed the land now that we're filling out as a family."

"Well, I'm not letting Clove go," Archer said with determination. "Mason may be a wimp, but I'm not. I know how to handle my destination."

"Destiny, Archer," Last said with a sigh.

"Same thing to me. I'm outta here." Archer left, sweeping all thoughts of his family from his mind. As far as he was concerned, he was going to convince Clove that she and the babies belonged right here. With him.

THE LAST THING Clove expected was how handsome Archer was when he came to pick her up. He'd always been attractive, but all dressed up in his best jeans and boots and combed hair, he was downright hot. She glanced at Lucy for confirmation.

Her sister's eyes were huge as she took in Archer's appearance. "Mind the fence," she said to Clove. "I'd be getting down off it if I were you."

"What fence?" Archer asked.

"No fence at all." Clove sent Lucy a warning glance. "Thank you for coming to get us."

"Thank you for joining my family for dinner. This will be a simple, quiet meal. Just what the doctor ordered."

Lucy followed them silently as Archer led the way to his truck. He helped Clove into the cab, then opened the door for Lucy. "Seat belts, ladies," he said.

Clove sat quietly, enjoying seeing the ranch as it went by. "It's very peaceful here."

"Yes. I'm sure Australia is, too. I've always wanted to go to Australia."

"You told me that once," she murmured.

Lucy cleared her throat in the back seat.

"Maybe you'd like to come see my house sometime," Clove said hurriedly.

"I'd like that."

Clove could almost hear her sister exhale with relief. She frowned, thinking it wasn't right to invite Archer to her home just yet. They had too much to figure out, and proffering an invitation gave off meaning she wasn't ready for.

"Here we are," Archer said. "The humble abode."

Clove got out of the truck, and Archer ran around to help her walk up the steps.

"I can do it," she said.

"I know. But you're not supposed to stress or strain anything."

She sighed. "I'm not a doll, Archer."

"That's debatable, Miss Penmire," he said. "Hope you like roast beef and mashed potatoes, because Helga's cooked that and a Yorkshire pudding."

"I'm dying and going to heaven," Lucy murmured behind them. "Real Texas cooking."

They went into the dining room, which was aglow with candelabra. "My," Clove said. "This is very pretty."

"It looks fancy," Archer said, "but don't get the impression we eat like this every night. This is the holiday tablecloth, and these are the special-event candles." He wrinkled his forehead as his brothers filed into the room, taking seats at the table. "If Mimi and the sheriff are moving to town, who gets Helga? Us or them?"

Bandera stared at him. "We don't know."

Mason shrugged. "Haven't thought about it. Miss Clove, Miss Lucy, forgive my brother's manners and allow me to reintroduce ourselves to you. Bandera, Last, Crockett, and me, Mason." He lifted a wineglass to Clove. "Congratulations on your pregnancy, and more importantly, welcome to the family."

All the brothers raised a glass to her. Clove blinked, not sure how to take their welcome. "Thank you," she finally murmured, picking up her water glass.

Lucy patted her back. Clove felt so guilty. The Jeffersons seemed so sincere, even though she had enticed one of the brothers under false pretenses.

Helga served her plate, heaped high with aromatic food. She nearly sighed with anticipation. "This looks wonderful."

Helga nodded, filling Lucy's plate. "Heaven," Lucy said.

Clove glanced at Archer. She found his gaze on her, watching her every move. "What?" she whispered.

"You're beautiful," he whispered across the table.

Everyone heard him. Clove felt herself blush, so she looked down at the napkin in her lap. As Mason began to eat, she followed suit, though she'd lost her appetite.

"How are you feeling?" Bandera asked.

"Wonderful, actually. Thank you," Clove replied.

"Good," Mason said. "Because we'd like to discuss some living arrangements with you."

Clove lowered her fork. "Living arrangements?"

"Yes. Now that you're here and expecting children, we'd like to make your life a bit easier. Less complicated."

He paused to look at her.

"Thank you," Clove said, wondering if she should be grateful or worried.

"Next door to us is a house you may have seen on your way up here," Mason continued. "It's the sheriff's house, but he and his daughter and her baby are moving to town."

"I see," Clove murmured.

"We'd like you to consider living there," Mason said. "We'd like for you and your children to have a place to call your own."

Clove's fork fell into her plate. She put her hand in her lap as she glanced at Archer. He was watching her, waiting for an answer. Clearly, he'd been in on this plan, too.

"Careful," Lucy murmured. "Think before you speak."

But Clove couldn't react beyond the angry astonishment she felt. "No," she said. "We already have a place to call our own. It's my home, and I don't need another one."

What they didn't understand was that she didn't want them to rush in and take care of her. Her feelings would be different if Archer had wanted her—ever wanted her—but he was obviously doing what he had to do to save face in his family. "You don't even know me," she told them all. "And most especially you," she said with a pained look at Archer. "There's just no way I can accept such an…arrangement."

They stared at her, completely buffaloed by what was lacking in their offer. She sighed. Lucy patted her hand. "Look. I'm a practical woman. I want the best for my children. That doesn't mean moving away from the people who love me, away from the land where I'm comfortable."

"I also want the best for my children," Archer said. "And I echo your sentiments."

Lucy and Mason stared at each other. "We've got ourselves some hardheaded ones," Mason said to Lucy.

"Don't look at me," Lucy said. "I may be eldest, but she's always been her own woman."

Mason nodded and bent his head to eat. The other brothers followed suit. Archer's gaze remained locked on Clove. She stared back, her chin lifted. Clove rose and went to the window. Lucy smiled, going to stand beside her sister.

Mason looked at Archer. "You've got your hands full with that one," he said. "Best of luck to you. You've finally met your match."

Clove turned away from the window. "Archer, would you mind taking me home?"

The men instantly stood.

"Are you all right?" Archer asked.

"I'm fine. Lucy, you stay here and eat. I'm going to go lie down."

"I'll go with you—"

"No," she told her sister. "There is no reason. Please stay and enjoy the wonderful food and company."

Lucy looked from Archer to Clove. "All right," she said, sitting down. "If Archer doesn't mind."

"Happy to be of service. Step out carefully this way. Wear my jacket," he said, laying it across her shoulders.

"I'm sorry to be such a party pooper," Clove told the brothers. "Thank you so much for everything."

"Are you sure you're all right?" Archer asked once they were outside.

Clove looked up at Archer as he once again settled the jacket better over her shoulders. "Archer, could I talk to you, just the two of us?"

Chapter Thirteen

Archer gazed down into Clove's eyes, seeing concern there. "Are you sure you're feeling okay?" he asked. "Maybe we overdid it. I should have made sure you stayed at the bungalow tonight. I didn't know it was going to rain—"

"Archer." She put a hand on his arm. "Relax."

His heart seemed to stop. "You worried me."

Her gaze stayed on him. "I really need to talk to you."

"Let's go." He led her to his truck, his heart pounding nervously. He kept his arm protectively under hers, steadying her on the ground that was beginning to slick with the light rain.

He wanted Clove to grow to trust him. To understand that he wanted to protect her. And he hoped that she could love him.

Because he was pretty certain he was falling in love with Clove. Fallen, more likely, since he'd felt ill when the cramping had started and he'd realized the babies might be at risk. He wanted Clove to be healthy, wanted her to enjoy this pregnancy she'd wanted so badly and which he now wanted as well.

Silently, they drove to the bungalow. Going inside to the den, Clove turned on the lights, keeping them dim. She sat in front of the window, looking out. "It's like a fairyland," she said. "So pretty here in the country."

"Yeah. Unless there's an ice storm. We get some of those. And once, a twister. This is supposed to be Tornado Alley, but luckily, we've only had one wild one come through in all the years we lived here. And one big, big storm, which nearly took out the town with flooding." He went into the kitchen, putting the kettle on for coffee. "What can you drink? What would you like?"

"Hot tea would be wonderful."

He liked her being willing to allow him to fix something for her. "You didn't eat much."

"I have very little appetite right now. I wonder if that's bad or good."

Shrugging, he said, "Probably fine, as long as you're listening to your body. When do you see the doctor again?"

"In a week. But I plan to be at home seeing my own doctor by then."

He dropped a tea bag into the hot water, his shoulders tightening with dread at the sure tone of her voice. "So is that what you wanted to talk to me about?"

"That, and some other things."

He brought the cups over, joining her on the sofa where they both faced the window. "I'm listening."

"I need to go home," she said softly. "I need to think."

"About?"

"About a lot of things, but mostly, what I've done."

He sipped his coffee, put his boots up on the ottoman and watched her intently. Her hair fell over her shoulders. It still held an occasional twinkling droplet of water shining among the strands. "I should make a fire," he said. "Hold that thought. I don't want you getting chilled. It's still nippy, like spring will never fully arrive."

Getting up, he stuck a few pieces of rolled newspaper under the logs that were already in the fireplace. With a long match, he lit the paper and replaced the screen. "I really enjoy this bungalow. More in the winter than in the summer, obviously. It's a great place to come when I want to sit and think." He glanced up at her. "How about I leave you alone so you can think? I know you've got plenty on your mind."

"No." She shook her head. "I'd be better off getting my thoughts out in the open. My conscience is killing me, Archer. I took advantage of you, and you and your family are being so nice to me that the guilt is overwhelming."

"You're overwhelmed because we're nice?"

"I'm overwhelmed," she said softly, "because of what I did. They say no action goes without a reaction, a consequence of some kind. My actions had consequences for you, your family, and even my sister."

He sat beside her again, certain that the fire was going to catch. "What has your sister said?"

Clove's eyelids lowered for an instant. "That her husband left her. About the time he found out I was pregnant."

"I see."

"Archer, I was really desperate and I thought I could make things right, but I made matters worse for everyone. And not only that, but I did it in a super-huge way."

He patted her hand. "I thought our family was fertile, but you're like a peach tree, popping out all over."

A nice peachy blush hit the tops of her cheeks, which he thought was kind of sweet. "Hey, it's a good thing," he said. "I like odd numbers. We're lucky."

"One would have been good," she said dryly.

"But three's something to brag about. It's like Poppin' Fresh Family. All that lovin' in the oven."

"That's exactly it. It's just outrageous!"

He laughed. "Well, I'm excited. You have to do all the work, and I get to be Instant Dad. Why should I complain? I see that my job is to support you and comfort you when you begin to feel like this ottoman has lodged in your tummy."

That earned him an eye roll. She sipped her tea for a second, then said, "Archer, if you hadn't discovered I was pregnant, would you have wanted to see me again?"

He thought about that for a moment. "I suppose not," he said. "You didn't seem too keen on me. I did come looking for you, but I didn't really expect to find you, and it's usually not a good idea to chase a woman who doesn't like you. The rewards just aren't there."

"I don't believe you've ever experienced that."

"No, not me personally, but my brothers have, especially Mason. It's not good when the love wires get crossed." He touched her finger, stroking her skin lightly. "I'm glad you're pregnant," he said. "It gives me a tie to you. A claim on you."

Her eyes widened. "Why would you want it?"

"Because I want a family."

"You could have had one with any woman."

"But you were so cute. And you set your big eyes on me, and I liked that, and then you were sweet in bed, and I liked that even more, and then you turned out to be remarkably fruitful. I can say, this is Clove, she's pregnant with my triplets." He gave his chest a solid thump. "Makes me look very studly. Potent. Quite moved me up in the brotherly food chain. Beat that, brothers!"

"You're crazy," she said, "and you're making all this up."

"No, ma'am. I truly am excited to be a father."

"I was planning to deceive you."

He put his coffee mug down, getting up to look out the window at the rain, which was falling harder. "Quit beating yourself up, Clove. I'm from a family that does things for crazy, sometimes inconceivable, reasons. I've met your sister. I can imagine you'd want her to be happy. It's not that big a deal. It would be if I didn't want to be a father, but I think I always secretly dreamed of being the brother to do something big. It's hard to make a statement in a family of twelve." He turned and grinned at her. "What else do you want to say to me?"

"It's just hard," she said. "Simply put, it upset me that your brother mentioned the house next door for me. Mimi's house? Is that what you call it? I don't feel right about having a house bought for me just because I became pregnant. I just can't accept it."

Archer nodded. "I completely understand. I would feel the same way."

"Really?"

"Yes," he said, coming back to the sofa to stroke her chin once with his finger. "I'd feel the same way."

Her eyes sparkled, and he decided he missed her without her glasses. "Your eyes are beautiful, but I liked you with your glasses. You were spunky like that. Why don't you wear them anymore?"

She looked at him shyly. "I feel more attractive without them. They're very bulky. I'm trying a new kind of contact lens Dr. Fern's friend recommended to me."

"Really?" He looked close into her eyes. "I can't tell you're wearing them."

"I am."

He'd only meant to look into her eyes and see the contacts, but now that he was this close, he could smell her perfume. He could sense her unease, which he found attractive, too, because it meant she felt something around him besides nothing. "I like you," he said softly.

"I think I like you more than you like me," she said.

"You don't act like it," he said.

"Be patient. I'm not very good with men yet," she said.

"You never let on in your e-mails. I would have thought you were quite the sophisticated Aussie with your stunt work and fun."

"I'm not," she said.

"I'm not sophisticated, either," he said, running one finger lightly over her lips. "But if you hold still a second, we can both practice." And then he kissed her ever so softly, and he felt so much better just having her lips touch his that it didn't matter that she hadn't fallen for him head over heels the way he wanted her to. All that mattered was that he had her now, and she was letting him kiss her—

"Oh, Tink," Clove said ruefully, moving away when the kitten patted playfully at her leg. "You little minx."

Clove scooped Tink up, her eyes no longer gazing at him. Archer felt a moment's tingling regret, and yet, he knew he shouldn't be pushing the limits right now. "You need to rest."

"I know. I think I'll turn in now." She couldn't look at him, instead she cast a worried eye at the door. "Do you think Lucy is all right?"

"All right?" He chuckled. "She's not that far away, and one of my brothers will bring her home when she's had enough of them. That could be any time now."

"Do you think?"

"Absolutely. Most people have a ten-minute window of patience around us."

"All right." She visibly relaxed. "What are you going to do?"

"I'm going to sit here and sip my coffee. Make sure the fire dies down and doesn't throw a spark out. Then I may sleep on the sofa until your sister gets here."

"Thank you," Clove said. "I appreciate you…what you're doing for me. In spite of everything."

"We'll answer all the big issues another time. Let's not try to figure them out at once."

"You're right." She smiled, the first time he thought he'd seen her smile in a long time. "Good night."

"'Night." He tipped his hat to her.

She disappeared into the bedroom with Tink. "Lucky cat," he muttered. Still, he was under the same roof with Clove, and for now, he'd be happy with that.

A man never knew when he might have a chance to kiss the mother of his children, and he intended to hang around for the next opportunity. It might arrive sooner than later, if he was patient.

Clove poked her head around the door. "Archer?"

"Yes?"

"What does Tonk do when it rains?"

"She's in the barn with the other horses. We put them up earlier."

"Is she warm?"

"Very. Quite content is that spotted equine."

"You're sure?"

He smiled. "Clove, the horses here are babied like you're babying that kitten."

She raised her chin. "Good. I was only curious." In a second, she'd disappeared, taking her feline with her. Archer grinned to himself. A woman who worried about a man's horse was a very good woman. And he liked her more now than he had even five minutes ago. "You're going to like being married to me," he said to the empty spot where she'd been standing.

CLOVE STOOD INSIDE the doorway with her kitten in her arms, looking at the big bed that wouldn't have Archer in it tonight. She thought about how kind he was and about how nice his brothers were being to her. She and Lucy had never known that type of warm acceptance.

Crossing to the bed, she sat down, putting Tink into the old hat Archer had provided for her. For a moment, she watched the kitten pick at the straw of the hat experimentally, testing her limits and her strengths.

Clove knew about testing her limits and her strengths, too. But now she wondered what would have happened if she'd just come to Texas to meet Archer, without a plan any more involved than simply meeting the man she'd corresponded with for two years. Would they have liked each other? Would he have been this focused on her?

She didn't think so. They probably would have laughed a bit, gotten to know each other better, marveled at each other in person, and then gone their separate ways. He would never have come to Australia to see how she lived.

It bothered her now. Having gotten to know him and having spent time with his family who wanted to buy her a house, she realized she had set the clock on fast-forward for a relationship that would never have happened without her pregnancy. Their pregnancy.

She had changed Archer's life and it didn't feel right. He was being a very good sport about everything.

She walked back out to the den. "Archer?"

"Yes?" He sat up. "Are you all right?"

"Please stop worrying about me." Hovering in the

doorway, she looked into the eyes of the man who she was trying desperately hard not to fall for. "In every good romance story, there is usually an evil villain to keep two people apart."

Archer nodded. "I know. I was just thinking how happy I am that Lucy turned out to be so sweet. She could have not liked me, you know."

Clove stared at him. "Lucy! Why would you think of Lucy when you worry about villains?"

"I don't know. I was worried she wouldn't like me, I guess. And that she might sweep you off back to Australia. That she might feel like slapping me for not taking proper precautions with you."

Clove's face scrunched with a frown. "Archer…Lucy knows what I did and why I did it. She's not proud of it, but she knows you had no part in what happened."

"Well, I did. Mason's real big on the condom song he sang to us as kids. You'd have to be part of our family to understand, but it goes something like this, 'Condom, condom, where's my condom? Oh, my gosh, it's gone to London. Without a condom, I can't play. Why oh why did condom go away?'"

He looked at her incredulous face. "The next verse is, 'Here is condom, at the store! Buying it is not a chore! Condom, condom—any color!—is my friend. Otherwise my freedom I will spend.'"

She stared at him.

He shrugged. "It's ugly, Mason's doggerel, but effective, believe it or not. The singsong quality of it sears into the mind so that we never had a chance to forget it.

He said he had to be creative for thirteen-year-olds, to short-circuit the raging hormones in our brains."

"You needed condoms when you were thirteen?"

"Nah." Archer sipped his coffee, frowning when it was too cold. He got up to put the mug in the microwave. "Mason believed in scaring us to death to keep us in line. When you're young and impressionable and all you want to do is kiss Missy Tunstine just once if you could catch her at her locker at school, well, that song unnerves a boy so bad he never makes the first move."

"I don't believe you. You're telling me a fairy tale, Archer."

He got his coffee out of the microwave when it dinged, and then held up a hand. "I am telling you the truth. The condom song was a deterrent in more ways than one. Hey, at that age, a guy is trying to summon a little courage around a girl. When you have to start thinking about your condom running off to London, you just freeze up."

"So you never kissed Missy Tunstine."

"I didn't say that." He gave her an eyebrow and maybe a bit of a smirk.

She sensed a challenge. "Well?"

"Luckily for me, Missy didn't have hang-ups. She caught me at my locker and smooched me so fast my toes curled in their boots."

Clove felt a momentary dislike for the brave and forward Missy. "And then?"

He shrugged. "And then when we turned fifteen, Mason put condoms in our Christmas stockings. It was all very straightforward as far as he was concerned. As a single parent, his role was to make certain we didn't get ourselves in trouble."

Clove hesitated, trying to decide if she should concentrate on the trouble part—a heading she fell under—or the rest of the Missy story. Sighing, she said, "So back to my point, which you got me off of quite effectively, I am the evil villain in this story, Archer. I've been thinking about it, and I feel we need some time apart to sort this out."

"No," he said, "I've never been more sorted in my life."

She shook her head, looking at his honest face and alarmed eyes. "You're a good man, Archer."

He set his mug down. "What you've done is give me the possibility of three children, Clove. I'm beside myself with joy."

"But with me. If I hadn't been playing the part of the brave and forward Missy, you would not have picked to spend your life with me. You would not have chosen me as the mother of your children. In fact, you would have probably gone off with a girl like Missy, into the sunset, a woman who made your toes curl in your boots and who understood life in Texas."

"I see what you're worried about," Archer said, "but you have to understand I like my ladies a bit forward. I like the fact that you jumped me."

"Well, I think that's a bit strong—"

"There I was," he said, his voice dreamy, "minding my own business, and here comes this little scaredy-cat girl, looking like she just got off the train from Lost and didn't have a ticket to Found."

"Archer!"

"And then she goes and gets dangerous on me, with a 'do and some makeup and heels, courtesy of the Never Lonely Cut-n-Gurls. I have to beat my brother off of her, practically, explaining to him that I got first dibs on the babe, even if she doesn't look like scaredy-cat anymore."

"I have never in my life been a scaredy-cat!"

He caught her by the hand, pulling her close. "You are scared of me, babe."

Chapter Fourteen

Archer and Clove stared at each other for a moment. If he wasn't so handsome, if he wasn't such a tall, well-built specimen, if he wasn't so manly, maybe she would actually believe that this man wanted her forever. But in the nerdy-girl stories she'd read, the woman had to stay beautiful to have her "revenge" by winning the man.

She was about to get very broad and misshapen. Slowly, she pulled her hand away from him. "I'm afraid," she admitted.

"I know," he said, "and I suspect it's about all the wrong things."

"I want to say, let's start over…let's see if you really like me, without the fact that I'm pregnant being part of it." Her heart felt very sad as she said this. "And yet, the babies are the best part. A miracle."

"That's right," Archer said. "And since I put them there, you should cut me some slack. I should be racking up points for good aim."

She tried not to smile at him. "I can tell that you are the kind of man who moves his way through life by making people feel better. A laugh and a smile are your emotional props."

"Yeah, but I can be serious, too. I'm feeling pretty serious about you."

They stood a foot away from each other, thinking about what was growing between them.

"And you know, I'm not just another pretty face," he said, coaxing a smile from her.

"Another story?"

"Yes, and this one's just as true as the one about the condom song." He pulled his shirt off, pointing to a scar on his upper chest, opposite from his heart. "This is where my twin, Ranger, shot me with a BB gun at close range. It was an accident, but it hurt like a son of a gun and I went boots over ass into the pond. My brothers had to fish me out, and then they had to hold me down so I wouldn't kill Ranger."

Her eyes widened. "That's a terrible story!"

"Yeah. I was lucky it wasn't a rifle or something. Mr. Misfire got grounded for a week by Mason, and we got the lecture of our lives on how firearms were to be properly handled before we put someone's eye out."

"Oh, dear," Clove said. "That tiny little scar does ugly you up a bit."

"Yeah," Archer said, "and take a look at this." He pulled his jeans down to the top of his underwear, where she could see a very shapely ridge of buns. Her throat dried out, and she stepped back.

"I'm looking," she said, "and everything appears to be in its place."

"But roll down the waistband a fraction."

Was he daring her? She darted a glance at him. He was staring ahead, waiting.

With trembling fingers, she pulled the waistband of his boxers down. His skin was smooth and medium brown, as if he'd spent most of his life outdoors without a shirt on. "There's nothing there," she said.

"There's a chicken-pox scar. I had one lingering, festering pox even after all the others were gone. My twin thought he was being funny and pounded it with a magazine. Mason then pounded his head."

"Gross."

"Brothers are gross. Don't you see it?"

She let the waistband snap back. "No." But he'd made her want to see more, and she had to resist temptation. Missy might have been a brave lockermate, but Clove had already thrown herself at him once.

"Huh." Archer craned to look. "I guess it is gone. I have a scar along my collarbone from where—"

She turned away from him. "It's not going to work, Archer. I will always see myself as the villain."

He was silent for a moment. "Will it help if I told you I like bad girls?"

She shook her head.

"All right." He passed her and put his hat on. "If I know one thing, it's that a woman who's made her mind up about something is fairly predictable. Like I said before, I don't want to go hunting where there's no game. Wise men pick the right spots for game if they want to eat." He went to the front door. "You do what you have to do to feel better, Clove."

And then he left.

She stared at the door, realizing that the pain in her chest was the price of her actions.

"I'm SORRY," Lucy said two days later. She and Archer stood in the barn, where he was tossing hay into stalls. "My sister doesn't know what she's thinking right now. She's been through a lot very quickly."

"You have nothing to apologize for." He kept his face averted from Lucy. It was just too painful to think about Clove. Never in his life had he experienced the type of pain he was feeling now. It never left him.

"But I do," Lucy said. "You know, I came here prepared not to like you. I felt that you'd taken advantage of my little sister. But then I met you, and I've spent time with your family, and you really are everything a family should be."

"We have our faults."

"I know. And so do we. That makes us who we are. But deep inside, this is a good family that's done its best. And so have Clove and I. The thing is, she's making decisions based on the past."

"Yeah?"

"Yes. She felt abandoned when our parents died. In her soul, she fully expects to be abandoned by everyone she loves. I've tried very hard to make certain she understood, when I married Robert, that she was part of our family. Of course, Robert's decision to leave is abandonment. But it's not her fault. Nor could she fix it."

"Why are you telling me all this?" He stopped pitching to fix her with a glare.

"Because you need to know. This is not Clove not wanting you. It's Clove not knowing how to get from one side to the other in a relationship."

He put the fork against a stall door. "Some things can't be fixed."

"Not by people," Lucy agreed. "Sometimes only by time."

"I don't have a lot of time," Archer said. "Those are my children your sister is growing. My psyche tells me I should be a father to them. I should take care of their mother during her pregnancy. I should see their first steps. These are not difficult concepts."

"No," Lucy said with a sigh, "but the two of you started off running before you were ready to crawl. Relationships take time. And healing."

"How much time are you suggesting she needs?" Archer asked.

"I can't say that. I don't know if it's five minutes or five years."

"Years!"

Lucy put her palm up. "Wait, Archer. I don't have the answers. I'm only suggesting that my marital difficulties and separation are hard on her. You'll probably be happier in the long term if you allow the dust to settle."

He sat on an old chair in the barn, thinking. "It runs counter to everything I believe."

"I know. You're from a family of fixers. Clove tried to be a fixer, and it blew up in her face. Then when she was feeling guilty, you tried to give her a house."

"That wasn't the smartest move, but Mason's pretty

obtuse when it comes to family matters. We'd just been through Last's paternity suit. It all worked out, but the idea that one of the Jefferson children might not be part of the family really tore at him. Hence the overeager offer to put Clove in Mimi's house." He pulled at his jaw for a second. "To be honest, it was a bad idea all the way around."

"Because you wouldn't have wanted to live next door to your family?"

"No," Archer said. "Because Last said it really hurt Mimi's feelings that Mason wanted to buy her house and land."

"Oh, my," Lucy said. "Does she like your brother?"

"There's some history there. No one's really sure what the history is, but it's always there, threatening to bubble up and boil over."

"I see."

Archer sighed. "And now Mimi's accepted the offer, but she told Last she thought Mason was a sap not to propose the deal himself."

"Ah. Sounds unhappy."

"And now Mason's even more miserable. He knew that if Mimi said she was going, then she was, and there was nothing he could do about that. Clove just got caught in his misery."

"Did Mimi want Mason to talk her out of moving?"

"I don't know." Archer stood, tossing more hay into the stalls. "Mason gets so worried about the Family Problem, as he calls it, that he gets tunnel vision. Family first, everybody else last."

"That sounds like Clove," Lucy murmured. "I've relied on her for that over the years." She sat straight, looking at him. "You know, I have a part in this, too. I should have realized that Clove would take my marriage problems as hard as she did. I should have realized from her job choice alone that Clove was trying to maintain control over unpredictable circumstances. Always pushing the limits to prove she could rely upon herself. I haven't been there for her as much as she's been there for me," she said sadly.

"Hey, it's never too late," Archer said. "You're sitting here, aren't you? Bending my ear?"

"Yes," Lucy said, laughing.

"Well, then. You're 'there' for her. She's just got to settle down a bit and realize we're all here for her."

"It's going to be the first time in her life she's had that," Lucy told him. "I've paid more attention to the farm than to Robert or Clove."

"Well, then," Archer said, "we're all just worthless."

Lucy smiled. "No, we're not. We just need to get to know each other more."

"I like you, Lucy from Australia," Archer said honestly. "Even though I was pretty certain you were going to be a big burr under my saddle."

"I like you, too, Archer from Texas, and if you don't try to be too big of a fixer, my sister may come around once she gets through freaking out over the fact that she's going to have three little bassinets in her house."

"I really, really want to be in that house with her," Archer said wistfully. "My boys are going to need me to teach them how to be men."

Lucy looked down at her fingers for a second, and suddenly, Archer realized just how hard it was for her to be having this talk with him. "I'm sorry, Lucy, about…your family."

"It's life," she said slowly. "At least I'll have Clove's babies to love."

He blinked. If his plan for happiness worked out, Lucy would not have Clove's babies nearby to cuddle and love every time her fingers yearned for soft baby skin. Her nephews would be on the other side of the world. "It's chilly out here," he said gruffly. "You'd best go inside and get warm."

Lucy stood, nodding, pretending that he didn't see her wiping away a tear. "Hey, I just came by to let you know we're leaving tomorrow, in case you don't come by the house."

Archer dropped the pitchfork. "Tomorrow? Is that safe?"

"The doctor says it'll be safer for her to travel now than later."

He felt himself starting to shake. A wall of realization hit him like a giant tidal wave he couldn't move away from, threatening to sweep him under and crush him. "I…is there no chance she'll reconsider?"

Lucy shook her head. "For all the reasons we already discussed, this is what Clove feels she has to do."

Archer stood, jamming his hands in his pockets. "I'm destroyed," he said. "Brokenhearted. And for some reason, slightly jealous of you."

She nodded. "I know. I would be of you if Clove was

staying here. I would be thrilled if she was comfortable enough to stay and make a home with you, but I would still be partially jealous of all you brothers getting to love my babies."

"And still I think you're awesome," Archer said. "Clove is lucky to have you for a big sister. If you decide you want us to come over there and give Robert a good ol' fashioned sense-whomping, just say the word and we'll load up."

Lucy smiled. "Thanks. Keep your passport updated. For now, I must admit to being the one who needed some sense-whomping. But Clove shouldn't have to pay for my errors."

Archer shrugged. "We all pay. It's family legal tender, emotional when spent and harmful when saved."

"Wow," Lucy said. "You're really deep. Did you ever think of becoming a writer?"

"Believe it or not," Archer said, "my writing is what brought me to this place. Now I can only hope to write a decent ending."

"Goodbye," Lucy said. "Good luck."

"Thanks," Archer said, his heart sunk so low he didn't think it would ever fill his chest again. "I can tell I'm going to need it."

Chapter Fifteen

One week later

Archer stared at the computer screen, realizing he had an e-mail from Clove. He clicked on it swiftly.

Hi, TexasArcher. Actually it feels pretty silly to call you that now, since I know you. Anyway, I just wanted you to know that Lucy and I arrived home safely and everything is fine.

He swallowed, his fingers hovering over the keyboard. Finally, he wrote:

Hey AussieClove. It's fine to call me that since we might as well go back to who we were. Sometimes starting from the beginning is good. Glad your trip went well. Take care of yourself and drop me a line every once in a while.

His fingers trembled as he wrote the words. They were the hardest lines he'd ever written. He meant them, but mostly, he wanted to say, *Please come back. We could work things out.*

But he knew he couldn't type that. Shutting off the computer, he went to find Mason. "Mason," he said when he reached his brother's office, "we go about things south of sensible sometimes."

Mason sighed. "Is that a news flash?"

"No."

"So why are you bringing it to my attention now?" Mason looked over a pair of glasses at Archer.

Archer gaped at his brother. "When did you start wearing glasses?"

"Since I got old," Mason snapped. "And that's not a news flash, either."

Archer shrugged, taking a seat across from Mason's desk. "How's the finances?"

"We're good. We're in the black. In spite of my fears of losing some productivity, being down brothers, we're actually moving forward. Some of our investments panned out nicely. Adding Mimi's farm to our land is going to be a good thing. We need to consider doing some crops on her portion. Maybe a bed-and-breakfast outfit, if we raise Helga's salary and hire her some help. I have lots of ideas for profit that we should discuss later, after I finish going over these projections. With careful planning, our children will have a healthy ranch to run if they're interested."

"Our children?"

Mason colored up his neck. "I consider all children born into this family to be our children. Jefferson children. I am planning for their financial security."

"I see," Archer said. "There for a moment, I thought the new glasses were a symbol of some pending announcement. Since you're getting old and all."

His brother glared at him over the spectacles. "They're only for reading! The computer bothers my eyes."

"Ah." Very sensitive was Mason to his new eye issues.

"So, have you figured out a solution to your problem?" Mason demanded. "I'm not sure it's a good idea to let your woman just up and walk away like that."

Archer glared at his brother. "No more of a good idea than it is to let *your* woman up and walk away."

Mason glared back. "To whom are you referring?"

Whew. Of all the brothers, Mason was the nut least likely to crack. "Never mind. Hey, Last said Mimi's feelings were hurt over your offer on her land. Have you talked to her recently?"

"Hurt? Why would she be hurt? It was a perfectly good offer. Full price, in fact, which was sensible between friends. I'm sure the sheriff was pleased." He blinked at Archer. "I even gave her extra time to move out. I wouldn't want the baby or the sheriff to feel unsettled."

Archer shook his head, wondering if more was changing about Mason than his eyesight. "Last felt Mimi wished *you* had brought the offer. You two used to be pretty close."

Mason leaned back in his desk chair, pondering Archer's words. "I did not want to talk to Mimi about buying her house," he said, his tone measured and deliberate. "I did not want her to leave. But what is a man supposed to do if a woman decides to go?"

Archer stared at him, his heart beginning to race with frustration and realization.

Mason shrugged. "I decided to make it easy for her. That doesn't mean it was easy for *me*."

It took Archer a long time to process what his brother was saying. When he did, when he realized that he and Mason were in the same boat, their sails turned into the winds of heartbreak, he simply left the room.

One week later

From: Clove
To: Archer
Hey, Archer—I'm starting to get a little potbelly! Well, it's more than a potbelly, it's more like a pot. Lucy says I exaggerate, but since I've always been trim, I feel like it's a pot. I'm thickening up sideways, too, which is kind of funny because I always thought my stomach would go forward. The other day I thought I felt something move. Like little butterflies moving up my stomach. Isn't that crazy? Talk to you soon, Clove

Archer bit his lip, ground his teeth and forced himself to think calmly.

Thanks for the note, Clove. Glad it's all going well.
Archer

There. Mason would be proud of him for his cool-headed response. Lucy would be proud of him for allowing Clove time to figure out her world and how the babies and he fit into it. He had no molars left from grinding his teeth in his sleep and soon he'd be gumming his food like an old man, but hey, if giving a woman space raised the odds in his favor, then so be it.

Suddenly, another message popped up on the screen from Clove. It had been only moments since he'd sent his to her. Greedily, he opened it.

From: Clove
To: Archer
I have to tell you something strange. Remember when you kissed me, and I climaxed? I think about that all the time. Being pregnant makes me think about you that way a lot. Though I may have made a giant mess of how I handled things, I loved making love with you. That was the single most wonderful experience in my life, besides finding out I was pregnant. I wish I hadn't kicked you first—it wasn't very ladylike and wasn't an indicator of how I really feel about you. Clove

Archer took that note in for a long time. "I sense a thaw," he said. "This aloof-male stuff is rough on me, but Lucy's right. It's working. So I won't say that I can't wait to be inside her again someday and that I can't wait to hold her and kiss her and sleep with her every night. Instead, I'll say something else."

Well, you sure got my attention. Don't worry about it. Archer

He looked at his typing. The words lay in the box, seeming stark and unemotional. "Oh, well," he said. "Sister knows best." He hit Send and turned the computer off.

CLOVE STARED at Archer's e-mail, her mind racing. She'd sent him such an emotional note, which had been so difficult for her to write! It was borderline Internet seduction! And he sounded so distant. As if what they'd shared hadn't meant as much to him.

Maybe it was different for a man.

"What?" Lucy asked, coming into the room.

Clove looked up from the screen. "Sorry. I must have mumbled to myself."

"You didn't mumble. You distinctly said, 'Maybe it was different for a man.'" Lucy looked at her. "Almost everything is different for a man. What's the topic?"

"Making love." Clove pointed to the e-mail. "I poured my feelings out to Archer, and this is the reply I got back."

Lucy read it over. "Huh," she said, getting up and walking to the door. "Some men forget stuff easily," she said as she disappeared from the room.

"Forget easily!" Clove frowned. She hadn't forgotten him. But if he forgot her, then…that sort of proved what she'd thought all along. Archer wouldn't have wanted her, Clove Penmire, for the woman she was. Sort of like Last hadn't wanted Valentine after their one-night incident, which she had gathered from the bits Archer was willing to mention about the situation.

She missed the easygoing e-mail relationship they'd once had. They'd met by accident when she'd written to ask a question about farming, as the Jeffersons had a Web site advertising stud fees and other services for their Union Junction ranch. Archer had responded with an answer, and they'd found common ground to socialize about. But that was in the past, she realized. "Okay, babies," she whispered, patting her stomach. "I guess it's just us now."

IN AGONY, ARCHER WAITED three weeks to hear from Clove. When he did not, he packed his duffel and checked his passport.

"What are you doing?" Last demanded as he walked into Archer's bedroom.

"Taking a trip," Archer answered.

"Going to hunt some kookaburras and kangaroos?"

"Something like that." He was in no mood to jest.

"Wish I had your focus," Last said.

"There were extenuating circumstances to your situation," Archer said, his voice grim as he tossed a belt into the duffel. "My relationship wouldn't have survived Marvella's interference, either. It may barely survive anyway, and it doesn't even have a heartbeat right now."

"Mason's gonna pop a coronary if you never come back. This place is going from Malfunction Junction to Malfunction Ghost Town."

"Mason has his own dilemmas to stew over."

"That's true. So now what?"

"So now," Archer said, zipping up his bag, "if she won't come to my world, I will go to hers."

Last's eyebrows rose into his hair. "Does Mason know?"

"No. You do. That's sufficient."

"Mason's going to be upset," Last said, "especially since you worked him over about Mimi."

"I did not," Archer said, "work him over about Mimi."

"He's superticked. He told the baby this morning that her mother was stubborn."

"The baby doesn't listen. Nanette only cares that she has her uncle Mason's undivided attention."

"Have you ever thought it strange," Last said slowly, "and I'm reaching here, I know, but just generally speaking, that Nanette sort of sometimes looks like Mason?"

Archer sighed, looking up from his passport. "Last, stop trying to make everything perfect. As you can clearly see, nothing in this family is ever going to be a fairy tale."

"You don't see it in her nose?"

"That tiny chubby piece of skin that won't take on a real shape until she's maybe fourteen? Or do you mean the apoplectic face she makes when she grunts in her diaper? That's when she resembles Mason." He tossed the paperwork into his carry-on. "Gotta go, dude. Wish me luck."

"Yes, but luck for what?" Last called after him.

"It doesn't matter," Archer yelled back as he started his truck. "I just need good luck for a change!"

"Here. Let me drive you to the airport," Last said with a sigh. "You may never come back and then the airport will keep your truck and it'll be a mess. Or you'll come back in two weeks and you'll owe so much in parking you'll have to mortgage the ranch."

"Thanks," Archer said with a grin.

"Never too much trouble among brothers," Last said. "At least not more than usual."

ARCHER HAD BEEN THINKING long and hard about his arrival in Australia. He'd pondered calling Clove and letting her know, and he'd ruminated on phoning Lucy.

In the end, he'd decided turnabout was fair play. Clove had nabbed him almost the moment she'd stepped in to Lonely Hearts Station, complete with her plan.

Today, he was the traveler with the plan. Stepping off the plane, he marveled at the change in the countryside. Tired from his long flight, he was energized by the people and the atmosphere.

A taxi took him and his lone duffel from the airport toward the address he gave the driver.

Two hours later, the taxi dropped him off at Penmire Farms—and a more dilapidated place he'd never seen. Archer's jaw sagged. Of course, he was in a different place and things might be a bit more casual here; not everyone had a Mason to crack the whip.

But this…something wasn't right. In fact, if he didn't know better, he'd think the roof of the white-painted farmhouse was sagging. Squinting, he decided maybe his eyes weren't adjusted from such a long flight—until he realized that the chimney was missing a few bricks.

A window of the two-story farmhouse appeared to be cracked. The fence, which held in a few mares and geldings, was ramshackle. Mason would kick every one of their tails if they ever let the fence at Malfunction Junction get in that shape. And the flower beds that first Tex their brother and then Last so carefully cultivated were lacking here.

He took a deep breath. Okay, it couldn't be that bad. Most of the problems, hopefully, were cosmetic. The livestock and horses, it appeared, were fed and recently brushed.

Yet the farm really did have a run-down appearance. The bushes were tall and the grasses around the wide porch blew in the slight breeze. Perhaps this casual approach to the farm had begun when Robert left. Archer tugged at his hat, thinking. Clove had been very desperate and upset about Robert leaving her sister. Possibly she had known that two women couldn't run this place without a man. Men, actually. It would take a dozen men to whip this place into shape.

And he was willing to bet his little AussieClove didn't know a dozen men. Sighing, he decided there was no reason to delay the shock of his arrival. He went to the wide, white porch and rang the doorbell.

Clove answered the door, her eyes widening when she saw him. "Archer!"

"In the flesh. Returning the favor, as it were."

She stared at him, not glad but not shocked, it seemed, for him to be on her porch.

"Are you surprised?"

"That you're here, yes. But that you'd come here, not really." She looked up at him. "I'm not making sense."

"It's okay," he said. "I understand. None of it does."

She stepped away from the door so he could come inside. He did, his gaze instantly moving around the hallway, noting that, while it was clean, the run-down conditions extended to the house as well.

Clove looked embarrassed. Mortified. He sighed. No point in avoiding it. "So. I guess you and Lucy have been trying to manage by yourselves for a long while. And now that you're pregnant, she's trying to manage a lot more by herself."

She didn't reply.

"Why didn't you tell me?" he asked.

"Why should I?"

"I don't know. So I could help you?"

"You didn't want to come here," she reminded him. "What was I going to say? My sister and I are over our heads in this deal, and Robert hates the farm? We're five inches away from having to give up the one thing we've ever had, that was left to us by the only parents we ever knew?"

He was silent, thinking.

"Archer, this is the reason I knew it wouldn't work between us," she said softly. "You wanted me to stay there, live in the house your brother bought for me, and be happy. But you didn't know me. Not where I came from, not how I live. Not what Lucy and I struggle for, which shapes the person I am. You just wanted me to fit into your life. And while I appreciated everything you wanted to do, it would never have worked because you didn't know *me*. Settling onto your ranch would have been as big a lie as a woman putting on lots of makeup and curling her hair and acting sexy to catch a man." She met his gaze with pain-filled honesty. "Deceit is no foundation for marriage." Her shrug showed her fatigue.

"Is Robert still…"

"Gone? Yes. It's just Lucy and me."

"How are you feeling?"

"Large, strangely enough." She smiled a little. "I suppose it's normal with three. The doctor says everything is progressing and that it's natural to be tired."

"I wish you had told me that you needed help, Clove," Archer said.

"Archer, I wanted many things from you, but help was not one of them. Penmire Farms may not seem like much to you, but it means everything to us."

Chapter Sixteen

Archer looked at her. After a moment, Clove took his hand. "I'm really glad you're here," she finally said. "Welcome to Australia."

Slowly, he pulled his hand away from hers. She lowered her gaze, recognizing distance.

"Thank you," he said simply. "I made a reservation at a hotel in the city."

"That's thirty minutes away, at least," she said, surprised. "Why don't you stay here?"

"With two unattached women? It doesn't seem appropriate."

"No one cares here, Archer. We're too far out in the country."

"I care."

Her eyes went wide. "You didn't at your ranch."

He looked at her, and then she realized what he was trying to say. He'd still been romancing her when they were at the bungalow in Malfunction Junction.

Now romance was not on his mind. She blushed, her feelings hurt in some way she couldn't define. "Can I offer you some food? Something to drink? I'm sure you'd like something after your flight."

"I'd like something cold if you have it. But I'm not particular. Whatever's easy."

She brought him a beer, and he took it gratefully. "Thanks."

Awkwardly, she moved to the patio. "Join me outside. It's nice out here."

He got up, following her outside. Sitting, she watched him look over the pasture that served as their backyard.

"So, how long has it been this way?"

"Since our parents died. We try, we really do, Archer. Lucy and I should probably give up, but the farm is ours. It just seems that the more we do, the farther we slide back."

"I can appreciate that feeling. It's ranch life." Still, he gazed out at the paddock, and she could feel him measuring the work, the money, the effort it would take to get the place in decent shape.

"You're always a surprise," he said finally.

"How is Tonk, by the way?"

He grimaced. "Still keeping me off guard, too. I'm trying to teach her cutting, and seventy-five percent of the time she does everything perfectly. Exactly the way she should. The other twenty-five percent of the time, she's got a mind of her own. We differ on approach, and she's stubborn."

"You'll eventually wear her out of that last twenty-five percent. She knows who's boss. Not that she likes it."

"It's a very slow process."

Clove smiled. "See that Hanoverian out there? Fifteen-point-three hands. I got her when she was just a spindly, argumentative lass. With some love and lots of attention, and teeth grinding on my part, we worked out a training schedule. Go try her out."

"Right now?"

"Sure. Jumper saddle's in the barn. You can try the cross-pole oxer if you're in the mood. If not, the cavaletti will give you a warm-up. Her name's Encino."

"It'll be good to use the muscles I've been sitting on for twenty-four hours," he said. "I know one thing—if I'd known a flight could last so long, I would never have let you return here."

She watched him walk toward the barn. If he didn't want her flying pregnant, then he wasn't expecting to try to talk her into going back to Texas. Her heart folded up like weary bird's wings. Not that it was unexpected. She supposed they'd made their peace with what could, and could not, be between them.

And yet, something inside her must have wistfully been hoping for the magic they'd once felt to steal back over them. The lovemaking had been fun and hot and exciting—they'd been very interested in each other then.

She went inside to brush her hair. The mirror gave away the toll her pregnancy was taking on her. She didn't want to tell Archer that the doctor had said she'd probably be completely bedridden within a month.

If she told him, he'd be obliged to stay. She spritzed

on some light perfume and used concealer on the dark circles under her eyes.

"Why am I doing this?" she asked her reflection.

Because you liked him from the moment he first touched you. Maybe the moment you watched him ride his spotted Appaloosa into the barn. And you fell for him when he made love to you.

"And I've been kidding myself that my heart is not going to be very, very broken," she whispered. With a sigh, she put away her things and went back out to stand on the patio.

Archer had Encino saddled and was now walking her in a large circle to warm her up. In a few moments, he let her slowly navigate the cavelletis. She enjoyed watching him work the horse. One thing he would find, she thought proudly, was that her horse training was perfect. The saddle she used was kept repaired and clean, as was Encino's stall. The horses were cared for like babies, and she was proud of how well she trained them.

A few minutes later, he was soaring over the cross-pole oxer, with Encino showing her best jumps. Archer moved well, and Encino made it look like magic, landing on the ground lightly, almost prancing with the joy of being exercised again since Clove could not do it.

After another jump, he rode up to the patio. "Nice," he said. "You trained her?"

She nodded.

He patted the horse's neck. "I could never get Tonk to do all that."

"Encino's sweet. Perfectly mannered, a technical

learner. But you haven't had Tonk long enough to work out all the kinks. Be patient. Give her time."

His eyes lit on Clove suddenly, his gaze dark with intensity. "I am," he said, "but she's enough to try a saint."

Clove lowered her gaze, knowing that he was talking about her.

"I'm going to jump Encino once or twice more because she seems eager. Then I'll give her a hose-down in the shower I saw in the barn."

"Thank you." Clove turned away, heading inside and shutting the patio door behind her. Her heart pounded and her blood felt on fire. That look made her so hopeful.

Maybe, in spite of everything, he did care about her.

Then again, he hadn't replied with much interest to her attempt to tell him by e-mail how much she'd enjoyed making love with him. He was here, but maybe he'd come here for his children.

For a girl who'd learned that life had tough lessons, it was very hard to hang on to the fairy tale.

It was time to find out.

WHEN ARCHER WALKED BACK inside, Clove simply said, "I'm glad you're here."

He looked at her. "Thank you."

"So you like my horse."

"She's a good jumper. I presume you show her."

"When I have time. We don't do a lot. I get offers on her when I do, but I'm not selling her. I'm sure you're wondering why, considering the shape our farm is in."

"No." He shook his head. "Once you've put time and

effort into a horse, you weigh the options of starting over versus keeping what you've got."

She took a deep breath. "I'd like to talk to you about the option of starting over or keeping what we've got."

He sat down across from her, his fingers drumming on the lace tablecloth of the small patio furniture. "I'm listening."

"I figure," she said slowly, "that we're at either an impasse or a crossroads."

"Probably."

"I'd like to call it a crossroads and pull out a new map."

"Go on."

"I'm wondering if we should choose the option of starting over."

He pushed his hat back. "And what's wrong with keeping what we've got?"

Her stomach tucked a little. He didn't seem open to changing their current unstable relationship. Or arrangement. What was it, anyway? "Well, as far as I can see, there's nothing essentially wrong with what we've got, but I think it could be better if we start over. That is, go back to the beginning."

"When we were only writing each other? That doesn't work very well for me."

"No, I meant, back to the beginning when we… when, you know, we had our encounter."

He blinked. "Sexually speaking?"

She forced herself to look into his eyes and say, "Yes. Only this time, I won't kick you."

"Thank heaven for small favors."

Was he laughing at her? Clove felt she'd met him halfway, and maybe he should do a little more than be the stony, questioning rock across the table—if he was interested in their…whatever it was.

"So, are you asking me to make love to you?"

"I'm asking, actually I'm suggesting, that we go back to what we liked about each other, before everything else got us confused."

His gaze narrowed on her. "Your theory is that our best communication is in bed."

"Or a truck. I liked that, actually. It was all very romantic when we were under the stars, before everything got so complicated."

"So we're going to turn the clock back, start over, and rediscover who we might have been together."

"I…it's crossed my mind."

He nodded. "I see."

They stared at each other for a long moment, and Clove thought the silence was the loudest scream she'd ever heard. Or maybe that was her blood pounding in her ears.

"No," Archer said.

She felt herself go light-headed. "No?"

"It doesn't make sense. You'll hop out of bed after we're through and say, 'Oh, that didn't fix it after all. It's just going to be me and my sister and my babies, toughing it out like Scarlett O'Hara.' Well, I didn't come all the way over to try to communicate with you that way. We need to talk, is what I think. And I think we need to talk about how we're going to take care of these babies."

There was nothing for her to say to that. Lowering her eyelids, she waited for him to speak.

When she felt his finger take her chin up, she made herself look at him.

"Okay," he said softly. "I hurt your feelings and that's the last thing I meant to do. Maybe I'm not listening."

She pulled away from his finger, but kept her gaze on him. "Do you remember when I told you that, due to Tonk's posture, I could tell she didn't like you? That she didn't like the fact that you were trying to boss her?"

"Yes." He sat back in his chair.

"That may be your nature," she said carefully. "In trying to order the chaos in your life, you try to rule it. Only, it doesn't really work that well with horses. Or with women."

"So you're saying I'm bossing and not listening."

"It would be better if we had a fresh start, rather than trying to work around our fears. You've met my family and seen my home. I've met your family and seen your home. We know a lot about each other's worlds. We're at a point where we ought to be able to go forward, together. Listening to each other."

"I think I like it," he said. "And I am listening."

She smiled. "Thank you."

"Now let me be sure I have this right. As part of our new listening exercise, you want me to take you back into that bedroom and make love to you."

"Our ears would probably be more receptive to messages from each other after that."

"No kidding," he said. "I have never heard of sex as

a hearing aid, but I am a man. I can be open to new ideas. I'm not afraid of alternative methods."

This felt better. They were returning to the easy banter they'd shared in the beginning. Clove felt herself relaxing.

"But I can't do it," Archer said. "And I'm not just being stubborn."

She tensed again. "Then why not?"

"Because…I'm skeptical. Afraid, even, to use a word I don't use often."

"Afraid? Of what? I thought we covered all that."

"I am afraid," he said pointedly, "of hurting you."

"Because of the babies?"

"Precisely." He crossed his arms over his chest. "So while your theory of intimacy as an emotional navigational device appeals to my, um, baser instincts, my intelligence tells me that it's a bad idea."

"You can't hurt me," she said, "unless we did something on the kinky side and that's unlikely today. You've been flying for many hours, and I know you're worn-out—"

"I'm not *that* worn-out," he said. "Do you have your doctor's permission to be intimate? Because it's not an option unless I know the doctor thinks it's fine. And even then, I'd probably worry that the doctor was a quack, or that he wasn't familiar with triplet cases, or—"

"I talked to Dr. Fern, your favorite doctor," Clove interrupted. "She called here to check on me."

He sighed. "Ever thorough is our Dr. Edna Fern. Still a hideous name, though." He perked up. "Why were you discussing sex with Dr. Fern?"

She laughed at his glower. "In case the topic came up."

"And when would it come up, with me in the States and you here?"

"You see, if we spent more time communicating and being intimate, you wouldn't ask such silly questions," Clove told him. "Dr. Fern told me you were flying over."

"She did?"

"Yes, she did. She didn't know the time, and I thought you'd be here tonight, so you arrived too early for me to have the wonderful cake baked I'd planned. See the mix on the drainboard?"

He glanced away for a second to eye the laid-out utensils and cake preparations with some regret. "Who told her?"

"Last. He was calling to check on something for Valentine. Or maybe it was Mimi. Anyway, that's how fast the news travels."

"This feels very much like a setup."

She smiled. "Conspiracy theory?"

"I'm not sure who would be conspiring with whom."

"Anyway, Dr. Fern said you probably have about a month to think it over. That coincides with what my OB-GYN here says, too."

"What happens in a month?"

"I'll probably go to bed for the duration."

"Bed!"

She laughed at his expression. "Doesn't sound like much fun, but it is a fact. I'm supposed to keep these babies in here as long as possible for optimum health."

"Then we ought not jolt them about," Archer said.

"I believe you are afraid, and that's just not romantic. I've heard about father fear before. Do you know that men sometimes are afraid the baby will grab their—"

He jumped to his feet. "Clove, I am a rancher and a cowboy, but there's only so much information I can handle. If we're going to make love, then let's break out the…uh, I need to go to the store."

"For what?"

"Chocolates. No champagne for you, obviously. But maybe some body paint and Perrier. Things to romance you with properly, since I really didn't the first time. Roses. Some shrimp. Aren't we supposed to throw shrimp on the barbie in this part of the world?"

"It sounds good to me, but since I can tell you're anxious, and I'm afraid you'll disappear from sight if I let you out the door, I'm going to pull a Missy Tunstine here and lay one on you. How about you just come in here," she said sweetly, "and let me strip off your boxers before you strip a gear? I've never seen a man so worried."

"I wasn't like this before," he said, allowing her to lead him into the bedroom. "I felt in control before."

"Even though I'd kicked you?" She closed the door and began unbuttoning his shirt.

"Well, that was unexpected, but worth it in the end." He stopped her fingers, kissing them one by one. "Clove, I am afraid I'll hurt you or the babies."

"Well, let's try out the doctor's opinion first. If I hurt you, you can just say, 'Ouch!' All right?"

"Okay," he said as she smoothly removed his shirt. "If you hurt me, I'll just say ouch—wait a minute! Clove, hang on. This doesn't seem like a good idea."

He sat on the bed, a picture of depression.

She looked at him. Then she dropped her dress.

"Well, I *was* worried, but I believe we can work around it," he said, springing up off the bed to pull her down on it with him. "Come here, you," he said. "I am going to kiss you for a month of Sundays."

She pulled at him, tugging him closer, and they rolled over in the bed so that she was on top. His hands slid into her panties, then quickly reached to unsnap her bra. She tugged off his jeans, and they went flying.

"You make me crazy," he said, kissing her face and her eyelids.

"You make me crazier," she said, "and I like it. All those roles of responsibility wear me out. I want you to be the one thing in my life that doesn't demand me to be anything but sexy."

"Sexy as hell," he said on a growl, tearing off her panties. "If you want the bottom, call it, because I'm all good with you on top and I'm ready for duty."

"Shh," she told him. "Cowboy, it's my turn to please you."

Ever so slowly, she slid onto his erection.

"Ah, God," he said, "*thank* you for this woman."

She started to move on him.

His eyes closed for an instant. "I'm dying, of pleasure I waited too long to have."

She moaned, thinking that she'd waited all her life to feel this wonderful. He gently moved her onto her back, and she gazed up at him. "I like your method of communication," he said. "I like it so well I'm hearing what you're thinking."

That made her giggle, which he took as permission that all was well. He moved faster inside her, and the pressure built inside her to where she could only stare into his eyes. The communication they were sharing no longer had anything to do with words, just feelings.

She cried out with pleasure, and he held her tight. When she felt him climax, too, somehow she felt the spasms start all over again.

They lay against each other, spent for a few moments, before he rolled her to lay against his chest as he lay on his back.

"You really like me," she said.

For reply, he gave her a light spank on her bare bottom. "Listen, I'm usually a long-distance runner," he said.

"And I'm usually…oh, I'm usually nothing at all because you're the only man who's loved me." She popped her head up to look down at him. "So. I guess you shared too much."

"Sorry. I meant I'd do better next time."

"Yeah? And who was complaining?"

He chuckled. "Okay. I'm trying to be overly impressive."

"And maybe I like you just the way you are."

"Funny," he said. "I used to think that about you."

"And now?"

"Now I—"

"Yoo-hoo!" Lucy called. "I'm home!"

They tossed the covers up over their chests, lying

with little more than their eyes peeking out over the comforter.

"Clove?" Lucy said, coming into the bedroom. "Oh," she said. "Hello, Archer. I see you made it in good shape."

"Hi, Lucy."

"No jet lag, I guess?" Lucy called as she left the room, laughing.

He rolled his head to look at her. "Your sister thinks I'm after your body."

"And my sister better be right," Clove said, getting out of bed to pull on her clothes.

"So now what?" Archer asked, grabbing his clothes, too.

"What what?" Clove replied.

"Now that we're communicating better, when do we get married?"

She turned to look at him. "Married?"

"Yeah. You know. What two people do, sometimes at an altar with a priest before smushing cake on each other's faces?"

"Eww," Clove said. "I'll be forgoing that."

"Well, I'd be careful with the cake," Archer said.

"I think we should talk some more."

"Okay," he said, pulling her backward onto the bed and tugging at her dress. "I *like* the way you converse."

Gently, she moved his hands and got up from the bed. "I mean," she said, worried now, "that we should talk more. I don't see having a two-continent marriage."

"I don't, either."

"Well," Clove said, "then we have to talk. Real talk. There's Lucy to consider. And this farm. I just can't pick up and leave her to everything with Robert gone. You know how much trouble it is at your place now that your brothers have found wives and left things shorthanded. It's no different for me than for you."

"That's true," Archer said. "This is stickier than I thought it would be. We do need to talk more. But can we talk with you in this bed? I swear I think better when you're naked."

"No," she said. "Right now, I think we'd better leave our clothes on."

He grabbed her, kissing her deeply. "You still make me crazy," he said. "But that's a bonus in your favor, I've come to believe."

"Good," she said, "because there may be bad news looming."

"I figured," he said, following her out of the bedroom.

Chapter Seventeen

"So how did the meeting with Robert go?" Clove asked her sister as they joined Lucy in the kitchen.

Archer listened with interest, perching himself on a bar stool and watching as Lucy and Clove set about preparing the cake.

"It went as well as can be expected when two people realize they can't make something work, in spite of their best efforts."

Archer didn't like the sound of that. He looked at the sandwich and chips Clove put in front of him with appreciation but not much appetite.

"I am so sorry," Clove told her sister. "I wish there was something I could do."

"There's not." Lucy sighed and opened the mix while Clove greased and floured the pans. "He doesn't understand the business here and has lost interest in trying."

"Maybe…we should just sell out," Clove said, her voice sounding a tad broken to Archer's ears. "I know we said we'd keep our parents' farm forever, but it is true that Robert feels out of his element here, and maybe a promise to our parents isn't worth losing your marriage." She stopped flouring to look at her sister. "I'm trying to picture myself in your shoes. If it was my marriage in danger, I would probably go with my husband."

Archer perked up. That sounded promising.

"I don't think that would help at this point," Lucy said. "Robert wants to live in the city, and I understand that, but he also says that he doesn't want me to give up my family inheritance. That he would feel like he forced me to do it. He says we should accept that our lives are too different."

"Oh dear," Clove said.

Oh dear was right. Archer munched his sandwich, using Lucy's conversation to analyze his and Clove's dilemma. It wasn't hard to see Robert's point. He'd feel the same way, probably.

Yet, his stubborn head wouldn't allow him to accept that Clove and he might not be able to "communicate" their way to marital and familial happiness. Of course, he and Clove were expecting children—many children all at once—and that gave him extra impetus to solve the problem.

He drummed his fingers, thinking about Mason always harping about the Family Problem. There was a lot involved with making things work out between two people, let alone twelve. It made Archer appreciate why Mason always had a crab in his attitude. "This is a really nice farm," he said.

The women stared at him. Clove's eyes were huge in

her face as she hesitated in her pan preparation. "It's in disrepair," she said.

"And I can see where that would be frustrating to a man who wasn't born to rural life. But the fact is, it's a nice farm. If I were a buyer, I would buy this place in a second."

"Are you suggesting we sell?" Clove asked.

"I'm not suggesting anything. I'm merely eating this sandwich and dying for that cake," Archer said.

She looked at him uncertainly. Lucy watched him, too, and he saw the pain in her eyes. She really did not want to lose her husband. "So, how much is this about the baby problem and how much is it about feeling lost about the farm?"

"I would call it an even split, one feeding on the other. When you can't make anything work—that's what Robert said—you realize you might better pack it in."

"Jeez," he said, "I'm sorry."

Clove turned away, but not before he saw her glance at her sister in distress. Sighing, he eyed the tea glass Lucy set in front of him, feeling doleful.

He sighed. "I guess there would be no reason to wonder if you might have been better off with just the two of you in the house, in order to be a really intimate, married couple."

Lucy gasped. Clove stared at him, her expression looking as if it might wilt to tears any second.

"I'm only saying that married people could use a little space to grow one on one," he said hastily. "Please, please don't cry. I really don't know what I'm talking about. I was sort of theorizing. At our ranch, we call it talking out of our as—uh, hat. Talking out of turn. I should just sit here and eat if I know what's best for me."

They focused on him as his rambling wound down. Oh, boy. He'd stirred up a hornet's nest, he could tell. Clove was thinking a thought that had clearly never occurred to her before, and Lucy was wondering if she had put Robert second or maybe third in her marriage. It was time to take his own advice and skip the third-wheel routine. "Hey, I think I'll go check on Encino," he said, hurriedly snatching up his plate and glass to take with him. "I'm very good at chatting with mares, so don't even think about me. No worries, mate."

He sidled out the door.

Clove looked at Lucy. "As much as I want to bean him, I think he may have hit on something."

Lucy shook her head, putting the cake in the oven. "What difference would it make now?"

"I don't know. Maybe none. But maybe it's worth suggesting to Robert that Texas is starting to look good to me as a residence."

"Would you go?" Lucy was astonished.

"I'm beginning to look at the reality that it may be best for all concerned," Clove said. "The babies, Robert, you—"

"Archer."

"And Archer." Clove's heart did a funny flip when she said his name.

Lucy sat on the stool Archer had vacated. "How do you really feel about that cowboy?"

"Like he just spelled something out to me that I didn't want to see. He does a lot of spelling, that cowboy, and it's annoying." She took a deep breath. "But when I get past being annoyed, sometimes I think he's got deep thoughts. If I'd been Robert, I don't think I'd want to live here with my wife's sister and her three newborns."

"Robert was happy for you," Lucy said quickly. "As am I."

"Of course," Clove said, "I know you are. But if he was already feeling overwhelmed by the ranch, if he already felt left out because of the relationship between you and I, if he knew that the newborns would come first with you since you wanted children so badly…where did that leave him? I sort of see Archer's point. And, not to mention, I was always here. It's not that the two of you ever felt comfortable walking around nude, or… having private moments in front of the TV."

"Well," Lucy said, "I walked in on you today, so we're even now." She smiled a little sadly. "I want you to be happy. Don't think about what went wrong with Robert and I. There was just too much, I think. Now your focus should be on you and your new family. Trust me, Clove, you should make this work—if you want it."

"It was not my intention to fall in love with Archer." Clove looked at her sister. "The funny thing was, I did."

"Well, he's just so likable. You know? He's easygoing. He's hunky. He's loyal. He's stubborn. He likes you for you. Where in there is the downside?" Lucy asked. "I know none of that can make you love him if you don't feel all the right emotions. But if you do, you might think twice about letting him board a plane back to America without you."

Clove nodded.

"Well, this cake will be done soon enough," Lucy said. "I'll bring you two out a piece. In the meantime, why don't you go talk to him."

"I wouldn't know where to start. My mind is racing. I'm happy, but I'm afraid. I'm excited, but I'm nervous."

Lucy laughed. "That sounds like love."

"Yes, but what if we can't make it work? What if, in our best efforts, we can't figure out a way to bond our lives together?"

"Well," Lucy said, "there's always e-mail."

CLOVE WALKED into the barn slowly, thinking about her situation. About Archer. How she felt about him. And the babies.

She had to make a decision. Futures were at stake— everyone's—and they were all at the most important moment of their lives.

"Archer?" she said.

"Yeah?" He poked his head up over Encino's stall.

"What are you doing?"

"Brushing this horse. I like her. Brushing and currying relaxes me. Hoof picking, not so much, but I like it, too."

"Can we talk?"

"Sure. Sorry, Encino. More later."

He came out of the stall, closing it behind him. "That's a great horse. You did an awesome job with her. I'm crazy about Tonk, but she'd just as soon give me a hoof as look at me. Encino's sweet. She knows her manners."

"You were imposing yourself on Tonk because she was yours. You're relaxed and spoiling Encino, so she's responding. But I will admit that Encino has been a love to train."

"I'll bet. When I get home, Tonk and I are going to start off on a new foot. Or hoof."

She didn't know how to take his comment about returning home. "Just remember, you haven't had her as long as I've had Encino. Patience is key."

"You learned a lot about horses being at Penmire Farms, didn't you?"

She sat on a bench that was in the breezeway. "When it's all you've got, you tend to learn it, fast, and try to do it the best you can. I did stunt work to help pay the expenses, but as you can see, Lucy and I didn't do as well as we could have if given more time. When we were left Penmire, it was under some debt our adoptive parents had taken on, fully expecting that they'd be around to use the equipment they'd purchased." Her eyes grew dark with remembering. "They had wonderful plans for Penmire." She looked at Archer. "Once upon a time, it really was a premier place for fine horses. People came first to Penmire when they were looking for the best prospects."

"I'm sorry, Clove."

"It's all right. Thank you, though." She smiled at him. "You know that running a ranch is a make-or-break business. And we were two young girls, not knowing what we should have known about money. About life. About business. We made mistakes."

"Mistakes can be made even by pros. We may butt heads with Mason, he may be tight as a tick and hard as a stone, but he can run the business of the ranch. He does keep it successful. They say that family money generally only lasts two generations. I believe that if Mason weren't in charge of our ranch, we'd not see financial wellness past this generation. Not to mention that the eleven of us make mistakes all the time that don't help our financial status.

"So don't take it too hard, Clove. And I'd say the same thing to Robert, if I knew him. People think running a ranch is all pretty horses and fields of waving grain. It's *ass*-busting. And most of the time, heart-breaking, unless the right things happen."

"Back to those mistakes you mentioned—"

"You're not one of them," he interrupted swiftly.

"Thank you." She ducked her head, then raised her chin to look into his eyes. "I've been thinking about us."

"You have?" He sat down beside her. Together they looked out the breezeway at the beautiful evening, before he turned her face to his. "I'm almost afraid to ask."

"I need to be more aware of the effects of my decisions. I changed your life when I came to Texas, and I was only thinking about myself."

"You had a lot on your mind," Archer said. "Clove, you've been in a difficult situation."

"Yes, but it can get a lot more difficult if I don't stop being so stubborn."

"I am used to stubborn women. You and Tonk. Didn't you tell me to exercise my patience with Tonk because I didn't know her that well? I am willing to do the same with you."

She tried to hold back a small smile but couldn't. His eyes were so warm and deep that it was like looking into dark, welcoming pools. "I may require lots of patience if I am not too emotionally bankrupt the first generation."

"I'm pretty tough," he said. "I think I can handle one little Aussie gal."

"And three babies."

"And three babies."

"So I'm coming to Texas if you'll still have me."

He pulled his hand away from her chin. "I don't think that's the best idea."

"Why?"

"Because you'll always miss your sister. And she's going to be alone now," Archer said.

"It is true…but I don't know what else to do. I am trying to make responsible decisions! What are you suggesting?" She was almost afraid to ask.

"I don't know yet. It's going to take some pondering." He pulled her up into his lap. "You can't run this farm in the condition you'll be in soon. Bedridden and wearing a nightie. My favorite doctor's order."

"Yes, but," she said, trying not to think about the delicious tickling he was making her feel inside, "that means Lucy won't have anyone to help her. You know, we really are going to have to sell this place."

"I am afraid you're right," he said, his tone reluctant.

"It's certainly something you and your sister will have to talk over, but it doesn't look good, I have to be honest."

"This is all my fault," she said, feeling sick.

"This is not all your fault, Clove. We are not a product of our family's mistakes. We are affected by them, but we don't have to let angst rule our lives. Besides, I liked you. I let you jump me. That should tell you that, from the start, I was all over you like a stallion on a filly."

"You were not," she said, laughing. "You didn't even like me. I had to have the Never Lonely Cut-n-Gurls give me the Revenge of the Nerdy Girl treatment."

"And if you ever do that again, I'll…shave my head and see how you like that," he said, back to nuzzling her neck.

"I would miss your hair for certain."

"And I think you're beautiful just the way you are. When I remember you coming into that barn, with all your scared, cute little nerves and saying, 'Do you want to take me to dinner?' in that tiny little voice of yours, I just get chills."

"Fever?"

"No. Desire." He held her tight, letting his hands start to roam. "Did you ever watch *Grease?*"

"What good Aussie hasn't?" she said, giggling as his hands got more playful.

"My chills are multiplying," he sang.

"You are so silly," she said. "You make me laugh, and I so need that."

"But I'm not being funny," he said. "I'm crazy about you, girl. Let's play alternative personalities. You be

Olivia Newton-John from Down Under and I'll be John Travolta from the States."

She slapped lightly at his hands, which were getting too bold. "Goody Olivia or Black Spandex Olivia? Gosh, I couldn't fit into spandex now if I wanted to."

"Depends on how you want me. Letterman John or Greasy John? I'll let you lead the fantasy."

"Well—" She was just about to answer, when she heard Lucy calling.

"Here I am," Clove called, going to stand in the breezeway. One look at Lucy's face told her something had gone terribly wrong. "What is it?" she asked, heading for her sister. Archer followed close behind.

"Your brother called," Lucy hurriedly told Archer. "Last says Mason's had a tractor accident!"

Chapter Eighteen

"I've got to get home," Archer said after calling the ranch and getting Bandera on the phone. "All hell's going to break loose with Mason down. It appears to be a serious injury, and they've just taken him to the hospital."

He didn't say everything that Bandera told him. One glance at Clove's pretty face, all swelled up with worry and pinched between her eyebrows, told him that less info was a good thing.

Grabbing his duffel and checking for his passport, he said, "I'll stay in town at the hotel where I made reservations. That way I'll be closer to the airport for the earliest flight I can catch."

"I forgot that you'd made reservations," Clove said.

He wasn't really paying attention. "Yeah."

"I wish the cake was finished," Lucy said, "so I could send you off with a piece of it."

"It's all right," Archer said absently, glancing around the room to make certain he had everything. "Okay,

you two girls take care of each other, all right?" He
gave Lucy a brief hug and Clove a fast kiss on the cheek.

"Let me drive you to the hotel," Lucy said.

"No, thanks. I called the same driver who brought me
out here. He'd given me a card in case I needed more
transportation. Luckily, he wasn't twenty minutes away
from here." He looked at Clove, whose face still seemed
fragile with concern. "Take care of yourself," he said.
"I'll call soon."

"All right," she replied faintly.

A horn honked outside. "That's my ride. I wish
twenty-four hours didn't lay between me and my
ranch," he said, worried out of his mind. He was pretty
certain Bandera might have parsed some details to keep
him from going loco. "Bye," he said, with one last quick
kiss for Clove as he ran out the door.

His heart was in his stomach. Mason. If anything serious happened to Mason, they were all going to be in
a pot of very hot water.

Mason had been holding their family together for a
long time.

"Wow," Lucy said when Archer had swept out the
door. "That's a man in a hurry."

"You've been to the ranch," Clove said. "It's just as
much to them as Penmire is to us."

"Yeah." Lucy sank onto the sofa, her gaze on her
sister.

Clove shook her head, sitting down across from her,
thinking that the smell of baking cake would forever be
associated with Archer walking out of her life.

"He'll be back," Lucy said.

But Clove knew it was quite far to be apart. Difficult conditions. No real emotional cement between them. Just the babies. "I'm...not so certain."

"He'll call."

Clove's stomach shrank at the thought that it might be a long time before she heard Archer's voice. "I hope so."

"You could go there," Lucy said.

"Not now," Clove replied. "I'm not sure the doctor would clear it. Besides which, Archer as much as said he didn't want me at the ranch."

"Why?"

"Because of everything here."

"Oh." Lucy looked at Clove. "Me."

"And our farm."

"I see." Lucy looked pensive. "He didn't want me to be in Australia by myself."

"He felt like it would be hard on us if...that were to happen. That I would be unhappy if you were alone." Clove was very worried, and she couldn't deny that she wished she could have gone with Archer. "I'd forgotten he'd made reservations to stay in a hotel here. You know, we really didn't have time to grow together as a couple."

"It's unfortunate timing," Lucy agreed. "I should have vacated the premises."

"Don't say that!" Clove shook her head. "No one knew this would happen. And Archer knew you and I lived together. Goodness, when we were in their bungalow, his brothers weren't shy about hanging around us. And the night we had dinner at the ranch, you stayed up there practically all night."

"Now, that was fun," Lucy said. "You don't know this, but Last can balance a beer bottle on his nose."

"Oh, my." Clove rolled her eyes. "Archer is going to be so worried until he gets back to that ranch."

"Yes." Lucy patted her hand. "I'm sorry your visit got cut short."

"We seem doomed to have short bursts of acquaintance. Almost like e-mail—very abbreviated. And I thought we could go back to the beginning, to when the sparks first flew and we were getting to know each other, but you can never really start over, I guess." Clove went to pull the cake out of the oven as the buzzer went off. The cake, she saw, was perfect. "Once again, the family recipe is perfection. If only relationships were as easy to fix!"

"Tell me about it," Lucy said.

MIMI WAS SITTING in Mason's hospital room when Archer got there two days later. Her eyes were huge as she came to hug Archer. "You look tired," she said.

"You look tired, too. How is the old hoss?" He looked at his brother. Mason's eyes were closed, and he had various tubes hanging out of him.

"He's out of ICU, and that's a good thing. They care-flighted him to the hospital or he probably would have died."

Archer's stomach contracted, feeling as if he'd been delivered a kick by a bull. "What the hell happened?"

"We're not really sure because he was in the fields alone. That's the problem. No one knew when he went down, and so he bled a lot."

Archer glanced at her, worried about the sob he'd heard in her voice. "You should go home and get some rest. Where's Nanette?"

"With Calhoun and Olivia. Minnie and Kenny like to play with Nanette, and Barley loves her, too."

"All right." Archer went to stand beside his brother. There was so much pain etched into Mason's face. Lines he'd never seen before. It was as if age had crept up on Mason when no one was looking. Or maybe staring the Grim Reaper in the face lined one's countenance. "Who found him?"

"Last, thank God."

Archer nodded, putting his hand over Mason's. "Hey, bro," he said.

There was no response. But he really hadn't expected one. "Go home," he told Mimi. "Get some rest."

She came to stand beside him, giving him a hug. "I will. By the way, how is your lady friend in Australia?"

"Good enough." Not really, but it was a long story and he couldn't go into it. Right now, he had to think about Mason. He was beginning to feel quite crazed with his life divided into places so far apart.

"All right." She walked over to Mason and gently stroked his cheek. "Hey, you hardheaded mule."

Then she leaned over and whispered something in Mason's ear that sounded suspiciously to Archer like *Come back to me.*

She stood. "Good night, Archer," Mimi said, leaving the room.

"'Night." He stared at his brother. "Mason, I'm home," he said.

He thought he saw a flicker in Mason's eyelid. He wished Mason would wake up. Of course, the minute he did and was coherent, he was going to want to know if Archer had solved his Family Problem. And Archer was going to have to say no. That maybe it was unsolvable.

It hit him hard, when his mind embraced that thought. Some things were simply impossible.

And no matter how much he might want to change it, maybe he couldn't.

Two weeks later

From: Archer
To: Clove
Sorry I haven't written, but I've been staying pretty much around the clock at the hospital. Mason is finally looking like he may pull through. Hope you're taking care of yourself. Archer

Clove stared at the screen, blinking at the terse wording. She'd waited in agony to hear from Archer. And he sounded as though he was a world away, which he was, but emotionally just as much as geographically.

It did not feel good. Or right. More was wrong than just his brother. Unfortunately, there wasn't much she could do about it. The doctor had confined her to bed a week early, and a nurse was coming to her house weekly to monitor her and the babies' health.

She was beginning to get scared—about a lot of things. That Archer might never come back. That her babies might not make it. That everything she'd ever wanted might slip through her fingers. This family meant everything to her, and she so wanted Archer to want her, too. So she wrote:

I'm thinking about you daily, Archer. I miss you. Give everyone my thoughts and prayers. And please don't forget that I love you. Clove

THREE MONTHS LATER Archer awoke to his cell phone ringing in his pocket. Sitting up, he grabbed it before Mason awakened. Mason was slowly coming out of the woods, and therapists of all kinds were working with him. Mimi came by often. All the brothers and their wives had been by to visit him. The storm of Mason being down had galvanized the brothers into realizing they needed to work harder at the ranch.

Archer had slept in the chair in Mason's room so often he felt as if he and the chair had become one. "Hello?"

"Archer?"

"Yeah." He rubbed at his stubbly chin.

"It's Lucy Penmire."

He came completely awake. "Hi."

"Um, I thought maybe you'd want to know that Clove has gone into labor."

He jumped to his feet and ran into the hall so he could talk without disturbing Mason. "What? Labor?"

Swiftly, he checked the date on his watch. "It's only, wait a minute. How far along is she?"

"In terms of contractions?"

"No. Yes. What month of her pregnancy is this?"

"The fifth. Almost the sixth. Could be the sixth, depending on the date of conception, which—"

His breath tightened. "Fifth! That's too soon!"

"She did the best she could to keep the babies in. They're just too many and she's so small."

Dizziness swept him. "Did you say something about contractions?"

"Yes, she's having some, but the doctors are worried that's not a real good sign. They're going to perform a cesarean section very soon."

"Crap!" He ran into Mason's room, not realizing his brother was awake and listening intently. "Can they wait until I get there?"

"No. Twenty-four hours, even at the minimum, would be too long. I'm sorry, Archer."

"Crap! I'll be there as soon as I can. Tell her, tell her I got her e-mail."

"Like a while back?"

He heard the gentle reproof in Lucy's tone. But how could he explain he was never at home anymore? And that he was consumed with Mason's care? The ranch, his brothers, life… "Dammit," he said. "I swear, I didn't realize it had been that long."

"It's all right," she said. "But it would mean a lot to Clove if she could hear your voice."

"Well, she's going to hear it very soon." Archer hung up, stuffing his belt through the loops.

"Are we having babies?" Mason asked.

Archer whipped around. "Trust that the very mention of babies would bring the first light of interest to your eyes since your accident."

"You're heading out?" Mason asked, his voice very thin and rusty.

"I am."

Mason nodded. "What are we having?"

"Boys, I'm sure. Hell, I don't even know."

"Archer."

"Yeah." He saw his brother's gaze focus on him tightly.

"You talk about her in your sleep."

"I do?" He was shocked. Often when he slept in the hard old hospital chair, he didn't think he slept at all.

"You do. You yak about her a lot. It's like a nighttime soap opera. I've quite enjoyed it."

Archer shook his head. "And to think I've been trying so hard to make certain you're resting well."

"What else do I have to do but lie in this damn bed? I might as well listen to you ramble. So this time, fix it."

"Fix it?"

"You love her. Regardless of how this came to be, fix it. Life is short."

Archer swallowed, looking at his brother's face. He would never get used to the shorn patch of skin on Mason's head, where they'd had to go in to reduce some swelling. "Mason, I'm going to call Bandera and have him come stay with you."

"Good luck," Mason said. "Dad."

Archer blinked. "Oh my God," he whispered. "I'll be a father in less than twenty-four hours."

Mason grinned and closed his eyes.

It was the first time Archer had seen his brother smile since his accident. And it was all about becoming a father.

Chapter Nineteen

"Stop right there," Clove said as Archer entered her room three days later. She was sitting up in bed, wearing a pretty jacket. And at least her hair was washed and her face wasn't as swollen as it had been. Soreness was her middle name. But when that cowboy strode into her room, she stopped him with an upturned palm.

She thought she had never seen Archer looking so handsome.

"Do not take one step closer until you hear me out," she said. "This time I'm saying everything on my mind."

"Clove—"

"I am moving to Texas," she said, interrupting him. "You and I and the children are going to be a family when they get out of preemie care."

"Clove—"

"And furthermore," Clove said, "I love you. I have missed you. It's been torture without you. I know you had to be with your family, but from now on, I intend to be like Tonk. We are sticking to you like a Texas tumbleweed."

"Tumbleweeds don't really stick—"

"Archer, you're supposed to be listening. Those babies want you. I want you. I've changed my mind about Mimi's house. I will live there. I will live anywhere. Just so long as I'm near you."

He grinned at her. "Can I speak?"

"No. I'm certain you still haven't heard me. I know you think the only way we're ever going to communicate is by e-mail—"

She gasped as he opened a velvet box that contained an enormous diamond engagement ring.

"*Now* can I speak?" Archer said, beaming.

"All you want." She gestured to him to come closer. "And you don't have to stand over there any longer."

"Good. Because I didn't want to have to toss this across the room."

"You can bet I would have caught it. Archer, it's stunning!" She stared down at the simple emerald-shaped diamond. There was also a wedding band in the box, of channel-set diamonds. "I have never seen anything so beautiful!"

"I figured I'd better show up with something impressive for the woman who conceives and delivers three babies. It's three carats, one for each baby."

"Slide it on," Clove said. "Although I'm very swollen and it might not fit—"

"Aren't I supposed to ask you a question first?" Archer asked playfully.

"Go ahead." Clove closed her eyes. "I want to hear you say it."

He took her hand. "Open your eyes. I want to see

those gorgeous eyes, which I loved even when you wore those crazy specs of yours."

She did, smiling shyly at him, her heart beating happily with joy. "I love you."

"Wait," he said, laughing. "You're making me nervous. I know I'm supposed to make a speech here. A proper proposal."

"You stink at it, so I'm saying yes or we'll be here all night." Throwing her arms around his neck, she hugged him tight. He fell into the hospital bed beside her, careful to avoid her tummy.

"This is still my favorite position with you," he said. "And we're managing to try out so many different locations of being horizontal." He kissed her lips, slowly, softly. "Clove," he said.

"Yes?"

"Clove Penmire, I love you. I want you to consider my proposal. I promise to love, honor and hold you, through good times and bad. I promise to take care of you like a prize among women, because you deserve it. Will you do me the honor of becoming my wife?"

"Yes," she said shyly. "I love you."

"I know. That last e-mail you sent me was the clincher, babe."

She wrinkled her nose at him. "I don't believe you. You never wrote me back."

"I'm sorry. Life was crazy. But I will tell you that when I got that e-mail, and you laid out your feelings like that, I knew no matter what happened, you and I were going to be together forever."

"I do love you." She let him slip the ring on her finger. "It wasn't just about the babies in the end."

"The babies!" He stared at her. "How are they? How are you feeling? Are you all right?"

"Everything is fine." Clove looked at him with that tricky smile he loved. "You can go down to the nursery and see them if you want to. Baby Penmire #1, Baby Penmire #2 and Baby Penmire #3."

"Baby Penmire?" Archer repeated, wrinkling his face. "We're changing that right away! I'll be right back," he said, kissing her nose. "I forgot all about the babies because you look just the same as you did the last time I saw you. Except more beautiful," he said hurriedly.

She laughed. "You're doing good for a new fiancé. Nursery is down the hall."

He tore out of the room. Clove sat very still, a grin on her face, waiting.

A minute later, he ran back into her room, his handsome face stunned. "Clove Penmire almost Jefferson," he said, "those are girls in that nursery!"

The expression on his face was priceless. "Don't you like girls?" she teased.

"Well, I do! But I was expecting boys. Boys I know what to do with. I have brothers, for heaven's sake. But girls—girls are a mystery to me."

She motioned for him to come close, so he did. They kissed for a long moment, then she whispered in his ear, "We ladies are going to enjoy keeping you off balance," she said, "but you miscounted those bald heads, my love. There are two girls and one boy. You aren't totally outnumbered."

"Oh. Well. I didn't *really* care about having all girls," he said with an embarrassed laugh. "Except for their pink name tags, they all looked the same to me with their caps on their heads and mitten-things on their hands. I'm just thrilled they all have your beauty. I blew them each a kiss and they're all very smart, I can tell. And sweet. And talented. And guaranteed to be successful at whatever they do, due to their mother's intelligent, brave and sexy personality. When can they come home with us?"

"I'm not sure, but whenever it is, it's going to be to *our* home, yours and mine." Clove smiled, her heart full of love and joy for her fiancé who loved her just the way she was. Archer held her tight, and smiled, thinking that this woman, his soon-to-be bride, made him the luckiest man in the world.

It wasn't every man who was fortunate enough to marry a woman who gave him three wonderful children. "You're my angels," he whispered, holding Clove in his arms. "All four of you. As long as I live, my angels are going to be right by my side."

And outside the hospital window the Australian sun glowed golden, sending rays of happiness splashing across their bed.

Epilogue

The wedding was in Australia, and it was everything Clove could ever have wished for. To her astonishment, the entire clan of Jeffersons came down, bringing armloads of gifts, toys and well-wishes. She even met people she didn't know were part of the family, two men named Hawk and Jellyfish. And the first people who had "accepted" her into the Jefferson family, Delilah and Jerry, also arrived for the two-week "wedding vacation" Archer and Clove had arranged. Two weeks, they'd theorized, was the proper length of time for family to get to know each other since it took so long to fly to Australia. Delilah and the Jefferson wives said two weeks was just long enough for them to spoil the babies, since the honeymoon was being put off for a year.

The men helped Robert. They liked him, and they felt that the family farm could be fixed up in no time. Setting about with plans and muscle, they spent their time before and after the informal family wedding repairing fence and tack and teaching Robert those things that he'd never had a chance to learn.

This male tutelage, Clove noted with deep appreciation, seemed to bridge some sort of gap between Lucy and Robert. For the first time in a long time, they touched each other as if they cared. Their gazes lingered on each other.

"It's almost as if they're falling in love," Archer whispered in her ear at the rehearsal dinner. "I would never have believed that they nearly divorced."

"It's strange," Clove murmured. "Robert admitted feeling lost marrying into a situation that he knew nothing about. When we ran into problems, I think he felt powerless to help because he didn't understand the running of a real farm."

"There's a lot to it," Archer agreed. "But he's catching on fast. In fact, he enjoys it." He pressed his lips across Clove's temple as they sat together on the porch. "I think he likes having something to talk to Lucy about. And that he likes having the answers for a change."

"I wish I'd seen that before." Clove turned to took into her husband's eyes. "Thank you. Thank you for everything."

"I like gratitude," Archer said, "but I'm afraid I didn't do anything."

"You did," Clove said. "You and your brothers, and Jerry, and Hawk and Jellyfish, helped Robert, and gave my sister back her husband."

"Good," Archer said. "I like that kind of gratitude. You worried me when I thought you were going to give her my children to save her marriage."

Clove blushed. "She's my sister."

"And I'm your husband." He grinned. "And I'm never going to let you forget that."

"Good," Clove said. "Because I never want to."

They kissed, each of them in the moment, trusting and in love, and knowing that the family they were sharing was what their hearts had always searched for.

"I love you," Clove said. "Stunt work wasn't half as much fun as falling in love with you."

"I love you," Archer said, "and the three angels you've given me—"

"Are going to keep you hopping for the rest of your life," she said with a smile.

"Just like their mum," he agreed with a grin. "I can honestly say you gave me the adventure that I hoped for, and I couldn't be a happier man."

Twelve months later, in Malfunction Junction

From: Robert
To: Union Junction ranch
Birth Announcement
Robert and Lucy are delighted to announce the arrival of SKYLAR and ZANE ANDREW on Monday 26 July 2004 at 2.00 p.m. Zane, weighing in at 7 lb 1 oz, measuring 51 cm long; Skylar Jayne, 5 lb 8 oz measuring 47.5 cm.

Mum, Dad, Skylar and Zane are all doing really well.

Photos will follow in another e-mail.

Thanks for all your good wishes throughout the pregnancy.

P.S.

I would like to add that Lucy has given me one of the memories that I will cherish for the rest of my life. For anyone who has experienced the miracle of childbirth you will understand what I mean. Zane is just as much a picture of beauty as Skylar. There are no words to describe my feelings for the lady who has given me everything that a man could ever ask for and much more. Well, maybe I'm biased but I think she will do a wonderful job and that most of the babies' wonderful personalities I can already attribute to Lucy. I guess I want everyone to know how proud I am of Lucy, not just because she just gave birth, but for her wonderful qualities as a woman and a mother (hey, I *am* the new father, I can gloat). As a last and very important note, Lucy and I would like to announce that we are going through the final adoption process for two children, two sisters. This farm, thanks to you, is a wonderful place for children to grow up.

Well, I've embarrassed myself enough so I just want to say thank you to all of the "Jefferson Cyber Uncles." You all mean a great deal to Lucy, I know this because she talks about you all the time.

See ya,

Robert

Mason looked at Archer. "Emotional sort, isn't he?"

Archer smiled at Clove and their three babies. She did such a good job with him and the children that his world was complete. Tink scratched at his boot, and through the window, he could see Tonk grazing. Life was very, very sweet. "Emotional is good. You should try it sometime, Mason."

"So, is this the end of the Aussie e-mail correspondence relationship? Clove's happy here, and Lucy's happy there, and you'll split your time between the two ranches, and the children will have dual citzenship?"

Archer's heart filled with love as he watched his wife nurturing their children. "She's happy. And I found the one woman for me."

"Congratulations," Mason said, looking like the strong Mason of old. "I'm really glad to hear it. I remember being very worried about you and your mystery woman." He sighed, and rubbed his chin. "Now, call the rest of the boys in. We need to have a family conference."

"Topic?" Archer asked.

"Mimi," Mason said. "That little gal is driving me nuts with her run for the sheriff's seat! More to the point, she says she wants me to be her deputy!"

*The fun at Malfunction Junction continues in
June 2005!
Don't miss BELONGING TO BANDERA
(AR #1069) by Tina Leonard.
Turn the page for a sneak preview.*

Chapter One

Effort separates the quitters from the rest.
—Maverick to his sons when they wanted to quit
studying the great classics and read comics instead

"What I think," Bandera Jefferson said, "is that he who lives by the sword, dies by the sword. Ernest Hemingway, in a not too kind moment, if you ask me."

"What are you blabbing about?" Bandera's oldest brother, Mason, demanded.

"If Mimi wants you to be her deputy, you'll be the happiest you've ever been, because the path of the sword has always been your way."

Mason grunted. "Philosophical and annoying, all at once. And incorrect, I might add. Having a healthy respect for quotes doesn't mean you know what you're talking about." Mason put his hat on before getting into the truck. "Famous quotations are only useful if you abide by their advice."

"Where are you going?" Bandera demanded.

"None of thy business," Mason said, "quoting Mason Jefferson, in his favorite conversational tone, Butt-Outski."

Bandera stared into the truck. "Hey, you've got a duffel in there! Stuffed full. What are you up to? You can't go off and leave us again! We're bone thin on the ranch as it is. The ranch needs you. We need you." He frowned, staring at his brother. "This is because of Mimi and that deputy stuff, isn't it? Mason, listen. If you don't want to run for deputy, tell her you're not interested. Tell Mimi you'll help her with her campaign and that's it. No more adventures. Say, 'Mimi, our hijinks are at an end. You and I are no longer children.'" He gulped. "Quoth Bandera, from a trough of desperation, on an unseasonably hot Texas day in July."

Mason shook his head. "I need to talk to Hawk, and maybe Jellyfish."

"The phone's in the kitchen," Bandera said hopefully. "Or you can use my cell if yours is dead."

"Gotta be in person." Mason cranked the truck.

"A duffel means more than one or two days." Bandera's heart raced. What if Mason decided not to come back for months? He knew very well Mason was under a lot of stress. It wasn't just the ranch—it was Mimi, too. Love stunk, he thought wildly, recalling a quote from some old rock song. Mason had never retrieved his heart from Mimi's clutches, and this deputy thing wasn't sitting well.

"Don't you leave this driveway," Bandera said, "I'm grabbing my stuff and I'm going with you."

"No." Mason began backing up the truck. Out of the window he said, "You need to stay here. There's work to be done."

And there was a brother to lose. There wasn't time to call a family counsel, but Bandera knew an emergency when he saw one. None of the other brothers would allow Mason to go off like this, not with him acting all secretive.

"If you move from this driveway," Bandera said, standing up to his brother for maybe the first time in his life, "I will follow you in my truck. You will see me in your rearview mirror like a hound from hell on your tail."

Mason sighed, putting the truck in park. "You're an idiot."

"Sticks and stones may break my bones, but words will never harm me," Bandera said.

"And if you recite one thing while we're gone," Mason said, "I promise to do you some type of harm."

Bandera went off to get his stuff. In the hallway, he ran into Crockett. "I just discovered Mason in the midst of another Houdini," Bandera said. "Not much time to talk, but go out there and stall him, okay? Just in case he decides not to buy my threats."

"What?" Crockett looked out the window.

"Just go keep him occupied," Bandera said, running up the stairs. He tossed jeans, boots, socks, a passport just in case—

Last came in the room. "Running away from home?"

"No, but I think Mason is. He's got his duffel in the truck and he's heading off to see Hawk." Bandera threw a toothbrush into the bag, and dug around looking for other things he might need.

"Why?" Last asked. "Can't he just call Hawk?"

"Apparently not. Which is why I'm riding shotgun. Unless you want to go?"

"No, thanks." Last backed up. "I'll pack you a cooler."

"Thanks." Running down the stairs and crossing the lawn, Bandera jumped into Mason's truck. "Crockett, you're a good man."

Crockett shrugged his shoulders as he leaned his forearms on Mason's window. "I'd go with you, but someone's got to work around here."

Mason grunted. "'Bout time you did something."

Crockett slapped his brother's hat down over his face. Mason moved it back into position.

Last slammed the truck bed after he put the cooler in. "Here's snacks. Stop and get more ice."

"Jeez." Mason looked at Bandera. "We're only going a few hours down the road. Do you think you'll need much more survival gear?"

Bandera pulled licorice strings from his pocket. "I'm good to go on the road less traveled. Frost, of course, again. I really like the wintry old poet."

"Dammit!" Mason gunned the truck, making Crockett jump back and Last hustle to the side of the driveway. "I swear I'll strangle you with your own licorice. And then you'll die by your own sword."

"I can tell it's gonna be fun," Crockett called. "Goodbye, Huck Finn! See ya, Tom Sawyer!"

"Just a regular bunch of comedians," Mason mumbled as he pulled away from the ranch.

"So what's the adventure all about?"

"Maverick," Mason said. "Why else would I need Hawk and his erstwhile loony sidekick Jellyfish?"

"Jelly isn't loony," Bandera said. "He's existential man."

Mason grunted.

"So what does Maverick have to do with anything? What do you think you can find now that you didn't before?"

"Nothing. But Hawk will be better at turning over rocks and running through dead-end signs than I was. I'm hiring him. Or them. Professionalism is what we need."

"Whatever." Bandera looked out the window as they passed the miles of their ranch. "We have one pretty spread of land. I'm going to miss Malfunction Junction."

"We're only going to be gone a few days," Mason said.

"Well, I like my little corner of the world just the way it is," Bandera said. "Hey, look at that!"

Bandera craned his head to look at the woman on the side of the road, waving a large sign. She was wearing blue-jean shorts and a white halter top. If he didn't know better, he'd think the halter had black polka dots on it, *big* ones. His favorite. "Probably a car wash," he murmured. "Slow down, Mason."

"No," Mason said. "There's no time. This is going to be a fast trip. It's an information-seeking venture, not a woman-hunt. Nor do I need a car wash."

They whizzed past so fast Bandera could barely read

her sign. The blonde flashed it at him, holding it up high, so that he got a dizzying look at her jiggling breasts. White teeth, laughing blue eyes and legs so cute he was sure the fanny she was packing was just as sweet.

"Stop!" he yelled.

"No!" Mason said, stomping on the brake anyway. "Why? Why couldn't you have stayed home?"

"Her sign says she needs assistance," Bandera said righteously, although he really thought it had read, "I'm Holly."

"And Lord only knows we never leave a lady without assistance." Mason glanced up into his mirror. "I sense trouble in a big way."

The lady bounced to Mason's truck door. "Hi," she said.

"Howdy," Mason and Bandera said together. "Can we help you, miss?" Bandera asked.

"I'm waiting for my cousin," she said.

Mason was silent. Bandera took off his hat. "Did your car break down, miss?"

"No." She smiled, and dimples as cute as baby lima beans appeared in her cheeks. Bandera felt his heart go *boom!*

"I'm getting picked up by my cousin," she said. "That's why my sign says 'I'm Holly.'"

"I'm confused," Mason said. "And nowhere on her bright white placard do I see the word *assistance*, Bandera. Or even *help!*" He sent his brother a disgusted grimace.

"We haven't seen each other in a while," Holly said. "He might not recognize me."

"Okay," Mason said. "You'll have to pardon us. We need to be getting along. Normally, we don't stop for ladies holding signs, but we thought you needed help."

"Actually, I do," she said. "I could use a kiss."

Bandera's jaw dropped. "A kiss?"

"Sure. I'd like just one kiss before I leave Texas." Her blue eyes laughed at him, and the thought occurred to him that Mason was far closer to her than he was, and that was a durn shame if she wanted kissing.

"Why?" he asked.

"I'm feeling dangerous," she explained, "since I just caught my fiancé in bed with my best friend."

"Ouch," Mason said.

"Precisely. That's why I called my cousin. This is our prearranged meeting place."

"So you're running away," Mason said.

"I'm going on a well-needed sabbatical," she corrected him. "We were getting married tomorrow. I don't feel like hanging around for the tears. I have an itch to see the countryside."

"Actually, you have an itch to get as far away from your fiancé as possible," Mason theorized.

"You understand me totally."

"So about that kiss…" Bandera began, unable to resist.

"He should have been here by now," Holly said. Bandera watched her little lips bow up as she worried. What man would be stupid enough to cheat on lips that could pucker into a perfect bud of plumpness?

"Guess we should be going since she doesn't need a ride," Mason said.

"Not so fast." Bandera looked at her again. "Haste makes waste, you know."

"Who said that?" Mason demanded.

"Some wise man." He took a deep breath. "Ride with us."

She turned to face him. "With you?"

He shrugged. "Sure. Why not?"

"Why not indeed?" Mason said dryly. "We have nothing pressing."

"What about my cousin?" she asked.

A motorcycle pulled up behind Mason's truck. A large, ponytailed man got off the bike, walking toward them.

"Cousin Mike?" the woman asked.

"Yeah." He looked at Bandera and Mason. "They bothering you?"

"No," she said hastily. "They thought I needed help."

He shook his head. "Your mother's going to be worried."

"My mother understands," she said sharply. "She wouldn't want me marrying a man with the morals of a…bull."

"Whew," Bandera said. "Well, time for us to hit the road." He figured they should. She might be cute, but she had issues. "Too bad about that kiss, though."

"What kiss?" Cousin Mike demanded, bristling.

Bandera thought many men would probably want to kiss this beauty. "No kiss here."

"I was feeling the desire to rebound," Little Miss Adventure said. "Love the one you're with and all that."

Bandera blinked with appreciation of her recitation.

He reconsidered his fear of blatant seduction and capture. What harm could she do him with Mason around? She looked like a Holly. She looked like a Rosebud. Gosh, he was certain she could be a Gertie May and he'd still find her ravishing. "You probably get kissed all the time."

"I've never been kissed by a *cowboy*," Holly said.

Mason's eyebrows rose. "Bandera, I'm going to let you drive. I need a nap."

"He's not the kissing type," Bandera explained to Holly.

"No, I'm not," Mason said, getting out. "Excuse me," he said to the giant fireplug that was Cousin Mike. Then he crawled into the back seat of the double cab.

Holly's gaze roamed over Bandera's face as he got into the driver's seat. "'Bye, cowboy."

Bandera nodded. "Best of luck to you." Putting the truck in drive, he pulled away.

"Thought you were going to do it there for a minute," Mason said.

Bandera watched the rearview mirror. Holly was getting on the back of the giant motorcycle, after putting her helmet on. Even from this distance, it was easy to admire her nice long legs.

"I never kiss women who practice seduction on the rebound," he said.

"Not when they have a Cousin Mike attached to them, anyway," Mason said. "That seemed like a high-risk scenario."

"Wonder why her fiancé was such a dope. Why do girls always hook up with losers?"

Mason grunted. "I think any comment at this point

should be a sonnet from Wordsworth, but I can't think of one."

"Maybe Shakespearean tragedy." The motorcycle was coming up behind them, traveling at a good clip. It passed them, and Holly waved, her long hair flying out from underneath the helmet. "I hate tragedies."

"A runaway bride would be a tragedy."

"A runaway anything is a tragedy. Trains, horses, brothers. All four-hankie events." He was coming up on the motorcycle again. Watching it carefully, he passed, wondering why it was slowing. Holly waved at him, her eyes alight with mischief; she raised her fingers and shot something through his open window.

He snatched it from his lap.

Mason sat up to stare over the seat at the lacy white missile. "It's that thing the groom is supposed to throw to his merry men," Mason said, shocked.

"Whoever catches it is next to get married." He recoiled as if the satin-and-lace circle might fly his way. "I've known grown men who wouldn't be in the same room with a garter!"

Bandera met his brother's wide gaze in the mirror, his heart thundering harder than it ever had in his life. The satin felt slippery and unusual between his rough fingers.

"And you *caught* it," Mason said.

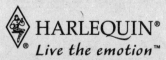

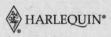

HARLEQUIN®

INTRIGUE®

**Don't miss the third book
in Cassie Miles's exciting miniseries:**

COLORADO
CRIME CONSULTANTS

*For this group of concerned citizens,
no mission is impossible!*

ROCKY MOUNTAIN
MANEUVERS

BY CASSIE MILES

**Available March 2005
Harlequin Intrigue #832**

When Molly Griffith agreed to go undercover to help out
a friend, her boss Adam Briggs wasn't happy with her plan.
Her investigation turned dangerous, and it was up to the
two of them to find the truth and each other. Would they
realize that some partnerships were meant to last forever?

Available at your favorite retail outlet

HARLEQUIN®
Live the emotion™

www.eHarlequin.com

HIRMM

Harlequin Romance®

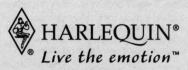

eHARLEQUIN.com

The Ultimate Destination for Women's Fiction

For **FREE online reading,** visit
www.eHarlequin.com now and enjoy:

Online Reads
Read **Daily** and **Weekly** chapters from
our Internet-exclusive stories by your
favorite authors.

Interactive Novels
Cast your vote to help decide how these
stories unfold...then stay tuned!

Quick Reads
For shorter romantic reads, try our
collection of Poems, Toasts, & More!

Online Read Library
Miss one of our online reads?
Come here to catch up!

Reading Groups
Discuss, share and rave with other
community members!

For great reading online,
visit www.eHarlequin.com today!

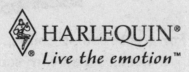

Curl up and have a

Heart *to* Heart

with

Harlequin Romance®

Just like having a heart-to-heart
with your best friend, these stories
will take you from laughter to tears
and back again. So heartwarming
and emotional you'll want to
have some tissues handy!

Next month Harlequin is thrilled to bring you
Natasha Oakley's first book for Harlequin Romance:

For Our Children's Sake (#3838),
on sale March 2005

Then watch out for....

A Family For Keeps (#3843),
by Lucy Gordon, on sale May 2005

Available wherever Harlequin books are sold.

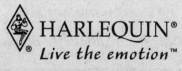

HARLEQUIN®

Live the emotion™

www.eHarlequin.com

HRHTH